I0554080

Forever Wyld

by

Laura Strickland

The Wylder West

This is a work of fiction. Names, characters, places, and incidents are either the product of the author's imagination or are used fictitiously, and any resemblance to actual persons living or dead, business establishments, events, or locales, is entirely coincidental.

Forever Wyld

COPYRIGHT © 2021 by Laura Strickland

All rights reserved. No part of this book may be used or reproduced in any manner whatsoever without written permission of the author or The Wild Rose Press, Inc. except in the case of brief quotations embodied in critical articles or reviews.
Contact Information: info@thewildrosepress.com

Cover Art by *Tina Lynn Stout*

The Wild Rose Press, Inc.
PO Box 708
Adams Basin, NY 14410-0708
Visit us at www.thewildrosepress.com

Publishing History
First Edition, 2021
Digital ISBN 978-1-5092-3831-6
Trade Paperback ISBN 978-1-5092-3909-2

The Wylder West
Published in the United States of America

Now she inspected this man in front of her and wondered who he was. Not a young man, by any means, he wore a battered hat and had a gun strapped to his side. A heavy coat covered bulky shoulders, a strong figure of just above average height. His hair, gone to silver, matched a pair of lengthy sideburns and a fine moustache. He had a weathered face and some of the bluest eyes she'd ever seen.

"Well, now." He placed an elbow on top of the piano and leaned, effectively screening her from the room and affording a few minutes of blessed relief. "That would be a shame—you leavin', I mean."

"It would not. They hate my playing." She gathered up a raft of music sheets in front of her. "That has been made abundantly clear. I'd better just admit it and…and slink away like a kicked dog."

He cocked his head. "You the kind of woman who gives up easy?" The bright blue gaze slid over her face. "Got to admit, you don't look it."

"This stint has been anything but easy, Mr.—"

"Hanson. Earl Hanson." He stuck out his hand. "And you are—?"

"Victoria Major." She had no choice but to slip her fingers into his hand, which felt broad and horny. She wondered if he'd heard that cowhand call her a hag. The second time that had happened in the past five days. Then she wondered why she cared what he'd heard.

Just another man in this accursed town. Did it matter what Earl Hanson thought of her?

Praise for Laura Strickland

"Laura Strickland has created a twisted tale that she untangles and lays out for her readers to soak in and swoon over. This is the type of story you'll want to read again and again."

~Author Sandra Dailey

~*~

"You are cheering for the hero and heroine all through the book and hoping the conflict will finally ease so they can be together."

~Author Jane Lewis

Chapter One

Wylder, Wyoming Territory, February 1879

"Sheriff Hanson? Sheriff Hanson!"

The call came from behind Earl Hanson and chased him down Wylder Street the way the cold February wind did, as piercing as a bullet from a Colt .45. In truth, it couldn't be classified as a *call* so much as a screech that caused him to flinch and draw his head down between his shoulders, like a man expecting a blow.

Oh Lord, he thought. Just what he needed today, when he was feeling lower than a snake's belly, and unfit for human companionship—Eulalia Culpepper, widow of this town and one of the least appealing women he'd ever known.

She seemed to be everywhere he went lately, or nearly everywhere—the mercantile, when he stopped in for a measure of baccy for his pipe. At Jake's where he went for a meal, and at the bakery, when he decided to treat himself to a slice of Mrs. Standish's pie. Her appearance caused terrible curse words to crowd his mind and, sometimes, cross his lips. It made him want to run and hide—maybe till spring.

But he couldn't run, not with his damned knees in their present condition. A lifetime spent in the saddle and endless days stomping the streets of this town had

1

done dire things to his body—things that, as a young man, he never could have imagined. Now, at fifty-six, he despaired of ever again feeling that pure surge of life and well-being that used to fill him.

Old and used up, that was Earl Hanson. And pursued by a shrieking harridan.

He forced himself to stop walking and turn around in the street. In days past, he'd faced plenty of dangers. Desperate outlaws thinking to shoot their way out of arrest. Drunken cowhands. Even a grizzly once, planning to move into town.

None of them had been one whit as terrifying as Eulalia Culpepper. But a man drew on his mettle, right? And faced such hideous perils.

She steamed up to him like a train at full bore, trailing scent instead of steam. Even before she reached him, his nose wrinkled in distaste. Never let it be doubted, Earl Hanson liked the fragrance of a woman, and he'd had his share, back in his youth. But what was this smell? Lilac? Violet? No, something far sweeter and more noxious.

He steeled himself further as she puffed up. She wore a cloak with a fox stole wrapped over the shoulders—foolish thing, and pity the poor animal that died for this woman's conceit. It still wore its head and delicate little paws, its expression pretty well expressing Earl's emotions at this moment.

Eulalia also wore a ridiculous hat that threatened to blow off in the wind. Beneath it, her red hair lay stiff as a helmet. Earl had a particular attraction to a redheaded woman. Fiery, they were and, as he'd discovered more than once, what might be called unbridled in bed. But Lord, he didn't even want to think about bed in conjunction with the widow Culpepper.

Stout and impossible to move as a wagon full of ore she was, a lot of her weight carried in her face, and with a bosom like a shelf. She had hard eyes, like two blue marbles, and that voice! He swore it could penetrate solid rock.

"Sheriff Hanson, how nice to see you," she declared, employing it the way a donkey might.

"Ma'am." Earl touched the brim of his hat and tried to escape her sharp gaze. "Surely you remember I'm no longer sheriff." He'd retired over a month ago, and after looking forward to it for years, was finding the adjustment harder than he'd ever imagined. Accustomed to being busy, and useful, he now found his days particularly hard to fill. His body might have given out. His spirit, it seemed, was still willing.

"Surely, I do," she sniped back at him, a terrible smile curling her tight lips. Was she trying to appear coy? Lord preserve him! "Isn't that the very reason I've been trying to catch a word with you this past week?"

"Ma'am?" He made it an inquiry, wishing he could disappear.

"I have a business proposition for you. Come down to the boarding house with me. I'll give you some coffee, and an explanation."

The boarding house meant Culpepper's, the place she'd been operating here in town since her husband died, quite a few years ago now. Poor man—he'd been tired and downtrodden. Death had likely been the best way out.

"Thank you, ma'am, for the kind invitation, but I'm—er—busy at the moment." A bald-faced lie, was that. Earl Hanson was anything but busy these days.

"You still living at that cabin of yours?" she demanded, ignoring his objection.

"Uh, yeah." If you could call it living. He'd been planning to build that cabin in the hills west of town ever since he could remember—to go back to his roots, so to speak. But now that he had the place, he still persisted in coming to town.

The new sheriff, Branch Wylder, was more than competent. Earl didn't have to worry about handing off his duties to the younger man. His head knew that—he still had some convincing to do when it came to his heart.

Eulalia Culpepper wagged a finger at him. "That's no place for you. You need to move back into town for the winter. Come down to my place, and we'll talk about it."

"Well, ma'am—"

Her eyes glinted like steel. "I have a room available for you. All warm and snug, and two hot meals a day."

Earl wondered madly if the room she had picked out for him was hers. His resultant shudder started at his toes and worked its way upward.

"You know the rooms at my establishment never stay vacant for long."

They seldom remained occupied long, either. Earl had spoken with plenty of gentlemen who'd stayed there and wanted to leave. Eulalia had all kinds of silly rules, from wiping your feet to being on time for meals. Only Tim Petrie from the Post Office had stayed—God only knew where the man got such stamina.

"I'm not getting any younger," Eulalia announced, and I'm a martyr to my rheumatism. I need a man around to help run the place." She gave him another look, one that, yes, could only be considered flirtatious. "Let's discuss an arrangement."

Unable to face that look, Earl fixed his gaze instead on that of the poor dead fox that clung on around her neck.

"I'm afraid, Mrs. Culpepper, ma'am, that would be quite impossible. I'd find myself another potential partner, if I was you."

She reached out and seized his arm. Standing there half way down Wylder Street, they'd started gathering attention from passersby. Earl saw Doc Coyote Sullivan pause with a check in his step, and give him a doubtful look before hurrying away like a man on a mission.

"Maybe I don't want another partner." Eulalia batted her eyelashes, an action so appalling it chilled Earl to his spine. "Maybe I only want you."

Two passing cowhands changed course abruptly, and a horse, tied to a nearby rail, blew air in distress. The ground might have rumbled beneath Earl's feet, but he couldn't be sure.

"Ah…" He freed his arm from her iron grip. "Mrs. Culpepper—"

"Call me Eulalia. And I'll call you Earl. I think that's proper, between two old friends."

The wind chose that moment to blow harder and tip the woman's hat off her head. Earl caught it, proving his reflexes hadn't all gone to pot, and crammed it back on her head.

"If I was you, Eulalia, I'd go right back to that warm house of yorn and take shelter. This is no place for you, out in the elements. As for me, I'm afraid I'm already in business up to my armpits." He edged around her, poised to flee. "But thank you for the kind offer, hear?"

"You remember," she shrieked after him as he walked away, turning heads all over the street. "You won't get another offer like mine!"

He sincerely hoped not. A man, even a hardened ex-sheriff, could only endure so much danger.

Chapter Two

The interior of the Trail's End Saloon felt warm after the cold wind outside, and smelled of horse, unwashed cowboy, and spilled beer, which Earl considered preferable to Eulalia's perfume. The place, which happened to be the oldest saloon in Wylder, was no great shakes. It had started out a low class of watering hole, been eclipsed when the Long Horn was built, and pushed even further down the pecking order when the Five Star Saloon started up across the way.

These days, the only folks who drank at the Trail's End were cowhands who'd been tossed out of the other places for brawling, cheaters at poker, and customers too ugly for decent company. Earl figured he pretty much matched that last category.

Anyway, he didn't want the good citizens of Wylder to see him slinking into the saloon in the middle of the day. Didn't sit right, even if he was no longer sheriff. And in his position, he thought as he bellied up to the bar, he needed a drink the way a drover needed a woman at—well, at trail's end.

Cody Muller, the bartender, eyed him in surprise. Earl didn't visit the establishment often, and rarely in broad daylight.

"Sheriff Hanson," Cody said politely. "What can I do you for?"

"You can quit calling me 'sheriff,' for one thing,"

Earl grumped. "I ain't the sheriff no more. See?" He thumbed his chest above the heart, where his star used to ride.

Cody looked abashed. "Sorry, Sheriff. What can I get ya?"

Someone joined Earl at the bar. A voice that oozed amusement said, "Get him a whiskey, Cody."

This early? The objection shone in the barman's eyes, but he wisely didn't voice it, and turned away to fulfill the request.

Earl stole a look at the man beside him. Coyote Sullivan, a tall man, topped him by a bit, and yes, he looked amused.

"How'd ya know I wanted whiskey?" Earl asked him.

Coyote gave him a level, green stare. "I saw what happened back there in the street. Any man who just faced off with Eulalia Culpepper needs a stiff one."

Cody set the glass on the bar. "Doc?"

"Nah, not for me. I have office hours." Coyote clapped Earl on the shoulder. "Not a man at loose ends, like my friend here."

"Damn it," Earl muttered. He waited till Cody stepped away before he said, "That woman—always following me around. Every time I turn on my heel, she's there. What in hell does she want?"

Coyote stared harder. "You telling me you don't know?"

Earl shifted uneasily. "Says she has some kind of business proposition to do with that boarding house of hern. Seems to think I'd be interested—me being at *loose ends*, and all." Sarcasm rolled off him.

Coyote Sullivan leaned closer and said in a low

8

voice, "I figure she has a proposition for you, all right, Earl. But it's nothing to do with the boarding house, and it's likely to end up in her bed."

"Jesus!" This time the shudder shook Earl from head to foot. "Don't say such things, Sam."

"Just dropping a word of advice in your ear. I do believe the widow Culpepper's on the hunt. If ever a woman's set her cap at a man, it's that one."

"Je-sus," Earl breathed again. "Talk about a fate worse than death…" He tossed back the whiskey in one gulp and tapped the glass on the bar, signaling Cody for another one.

"You'd best keep clear of her," Coyote said.

"I try. Most assuredly, I do." Nervously, Earl glanced over his shoulder. "She won't come in here after me, will she?"

"In here?" Coyote snorted. "Doubt it. This place isn't respectable enough for her."

Earl thought about that while Cody refilled his glass. "You reckon so? Then this is my new watering hole."

"Here?" Coyote repeated, looking astonished.

"I reckon all I need to do, in order to keep out of her way, is turn as un-respectable as I can." Shouldn't be all that difficult. Sure, he'd spent the last twenty years or so acting as sheriff, the past eight right here in Wylder. But there'd been times, before then, when he'd broken the law, lived on the edge, and used the guns he still wore for purposes other than keeping the peace. "I think I can manage that."

Coyote leaned on the bar companionably. "I do hear tell you've been spending more time than usual in Wylder saloons."

"I like the company."

"But you're not ordinarily what I'd call a drinker."

"Never was." At least not until recently. "I've seen how guns and whiskey don't mix. But you tell me, Sam, why would that durned woman set her cap at me, of all men?"

Coyote pretended to look surprised. "Why, you're a catch now that you've built that spanking new cabin for yourself. And you're no longer risking your life on a regular basis. Besides—I guess you ain't too homely."

Earl gave Coyote a questioning stare.

Coyote grinned. "Eliza Jane"—his wife—"assures me of that. Apparently there's a number of older ladies, widows and such, been eyeing you up."

Earl groaned. "You hear me on this, Sam Sullivan—I've paid my dues in that regard, even as I paid them all those years acting sheriff. It's time for me to enjoy myself."

"And are you?" Coyote challenged.

Well, there was a question. The last few years, his job as sheriff had proved a trial to him. The territory he was expected to oversee just kept getting bigger and more populated. The railroad brought in people—and trouble, because as population increased so did miscreants. Wylder, as well he knew, wanted to be a respectable town.

It hadn't quite got there yet.

Anyway, once his body started showing the effects of a hard-lived life, he'd longed to be shed of his responsibilities. Though, now that he was…

"Sure am," he told Sullivan a bit defiantly.

"How's the new cabin, anyway?" Coyote was nobody's fool.

Lonely. Earl wouldn't admit it, not after voicing his longing to be off on his own and left in peace for a spell. Just him, that cabin, the trees, and an occasional critter that wandered by.

But the wind tended to moan around the walls of the cabin, and all the critters, so far, had been hostile.

"Tell you what," Coyote said. "You need to get yourself a dog."

"What in tarnation for?"

"They make good companions. And word on the street has it Eulalia Culpepper can't abide 'em."

About to bristle, Earl thought better of it. "You don't say?"

"I do."

Earl tapped his glass on the bar again. Now, there was an interesting proposition.

Maybe he just hadn't met the right companion, as yet.

Chapter Three

Victoria Major eyed herself in the looking glass with considerable trepidation. Had she dressed properly for the occasion? So wavy and speckled was the mirror, she could barely tell.

What did one wear to play the piano in a saloon? In the course of her near forty-eight years, she'd held many and varied positions. Clerk in a yard goods store. Assistant to a haberdasher. She'd even tried, more recently here in Wylder, a stint as a waitress.

Goodness, that hadn't ended well. She could still see the outraged stare of the cowboy when she dropped his dinner in his lap—a steak still sizzling from the griddle. Not on purpose, of course. The heavy platter had simply slipped out of her hand and done a somersault in midair before landing food-side down.

Oh, how he'd cursed! She'd never heard such words. The ones that hurt the most, though, had been those he'd howled in her face at the end.

"You clumsy old hag!"

Was she clumsy? Yes, when she felt less than confident. Right now, for instance, her hands shook so badly she didn't know if she'd be able to carry out her upcoming assignment.

But was she an old hag?

Earnestly, through the spotted glass, she stared into her own eyes. She'd been attractive, once. Long ago.

Never beautiful, maybe, but she'd had a certain something. A lovely, fair complexion that contrasted with her vivid red hair and pale gray eyes. A certain bloom, like a rose.

Now, as an aging spinster, that bloom had faded. Lines marked the corners of her eyes—from smiling, given, but they never quite went away. Even the color of her hair had dimmed.

No matter, she told herself firmly. Nobody would care how the piano player looked. She would be heard and not seen.

Her bedroom door creaked open, and her friend, Hattie Morgan, stepped in. Hattie's husband, Tom, worked as a cooper here in Wylder. As old family friends, they'd opened their home to Victoria in her time of need. Hattie had even got Victoria the job waitressing at the town diner.

She now gave Victoria a doubtful stare. "Are you sure you want to do this? I don't think it's a good idea. That saloon—"

"I have to make a living, Hattie. I refuse to mooch off you and Tom."

"Yes, but that saloon, of all places!"

"I used to accompany Father to drinking establishments, when he played." Like her, John Major had been a pianist, classically trained.

"That was different. Those were civilized establishments, back East. The Trail's End is like no place you've ever seen."

"How bad can it be?" True, the saloon had looked pretty rough when Victoria stopped in, inquiring about the notice placed in the Wylder Mercantile, which said merely, *Piano Player Needed, The Trail's End Saloon.*

"I'm just there to play background music."

"You don't understand, Victoria. There are nightly fights. Shootings!"

Victoria's eyes widened and her fear rose, threatening to strangle her. "You don't say!"

"I do. The patrons there are bad 'uns, or so Tom says—the cowhands and men down from the mountains who've been tossed out of the other saloons and can't drink there anymore. There are even desperate gunslingers. Billy Callahan, at The Trail's End, lets them in."

Victoria pressed her hand to her chest. "Goodness. Why?"

"If he didn't, I reckon he'd have no customers at all and would need to shut down. Victoria, why don't you reconsider?"

"Hattie, I have to pay my way. Ever since Father's death, I've done so."

"Yes." Hattie looked troubled. "Yet in the past your jobs were—well, genteel."

So they were, if oft times demoralizing and downright depressing. After her early turns clerking, she'd migrated into teaching positions at various girls' schools, serving as music mistress. But the last position had ended—well, in disgrace that still made her flush with heat, just remembering it.

How dared she think she deserved better than playing the piano in some low-class drinking establishment?

"Let me give it a try, Hattie." She tipped up her chin. "If it doesn't go well, I will reconsider. All right?"

Hattie did not look happy. But she said, "It's not up to me to let you do anything. You are your own woman,

Victoria."

"Then, do I look presentable?"

Hattie inspected her with a judicious eye. "You look very—respectable. Maybe too much so."

"Nonsense. How can a woman look too respectable?"

****

Victoria's knees quaked beneath her as she entered the Trail's End saloon. When the proprietor, Mr. Callahan, had hired her, he'd told her to come in the back door. Now he, along with the barman, stood behind the bar. She caught his eye from the doorway.

"Miss Major." As Hattie had, he eyed her up and down. Only this wasn't the way Hattie had looked at her, not at all. Mr. Callahan, a rather rough-looking character in his mid-forties, seemed to measure her body with his gaze, before fastening on her face. "Ah—didn't I tell you to, er, dress up a little?"

Victoria glanced down at herself. She had but two good dresses. The one she wore today was dark blue and buttoned all the way up to the throat, with long sleeves trimmed in lace. It might not be the latest fashion, but it had served her well in the classroom. She had twisted her hair up into a tight chignon, and covered it with a hat. "I did dress up." She gulped back her increased nervousness. "Is this inappropriate?"

"Well, now." Mr. Callahan looked unhappy. "Most women who come in here—and there ain't many, you understand—tend to dress a bit more...colorfully."

Victoria brightened. "I have a beige dress also. Would you like me to wear that next time?"

A crash came from across the room. Someone had turned a table over, and men shouted at one another.

"Just start playing!" Mr. Callahan waved wildly at the corner. "It tends to calm them down."

The high-backed piano stood in the corner at which he'd waved. Victoria had seen it the other morning when she'd come in to inquire about the job. Of course, the place had been quiet then, dead quiet. Not so now. A single, plank-floored room dotted with tables, it also boiled with heat and—well, to be quite frank, noxious odors, and gave the impression of bursting at the seams.

No one noticed as she slipped to the piano in the corner. A scarred and battered specimen, it lacked either bench or stool and had been furnished with a chair instead. Victoria sank into it, her knees giving way.

In the past, she'd made music on a variety of instruments. Spinets, baby grands—even full-size grand pianos flawlessly tuned. None like this. She wondered how it had gotten here. On a wagon? A railroad car?

She drew a breath and extended her fingers above the keys. What to play? In her experience, Chopin always went over well, and had a calming effect.

The piano hadn't been tuned in some time. When she began to play, the strings jangled and made a hash of the lovely nocturne. So noisy was the room, she doubted anyone could hear the music, however it sounded.

The old upright stood at an angle to the wall, and she had to crane her head in order to see what went on in the room. The argument in the far corner had grown louder. Mr. Callahan had gone over there, presumably to sort things out. At a table closer to Victoria, three cowhands sat drinking whiskey. Not far off, a woman stood talking to a man, her clothing so shocking it almost made Victoria fumble the keys.

Was that how women dressed, here in Wylder? Hattie certainly didn't, and she'd seen no other ladies dressed that way when she went around town looking for a job.

Scandalous. The woman wore a bright pink gown, replete with ruffles and a bodice cut so low it revealed—well, quite nearly everything.

Could that woman be a prostitute? Heavens! Hattie had warned Victoria there was a house of ill-repute in town, and that she should steer well clear of it. You'd think they'd keep such business to that location, rather than let it flourish in the saloon.

Abruptly, the argument on the other side of the room quieted. As a result, Victoria's efforts could suddenly be heard. Heads began to turn her way.

The keys tinkled beneath her fingers and the notes flew in an ill-tuned stream. It didn't sound anything like what she'd learned at her father's knee. Neither did it sound bad, exactly.

A moment of stunned silence ensued, when the place went so quiet she could nearly hear her own heartbeat. Then one of the three cowhands at the nearest table rose and turned toward Victoria, his face like a thundercloud.

"What in holy tarnation is that hogs' wallop?"

Chapter Four

Victoria's hands froze above the keys, and a tidal wave of dismay rushed over her. There, pinioned behind the piano and suddenly the focus of all eyes, she did not know what to say.

The expression on the cowhand's face was—well, she had no words for that either. Except, maybe, outraged. Disparaging. And mightily displeased, as if Victoria had done something to personally offend him.

Someone tittered. It was the woman in the bright pink dress. Victoria found her face among the many, and recognized the look there. So had she been regarded all too often by other women, in the past.

Mr. Callahan came hurrying over from behind the bar and no, he didn't look pleased either. But he imposed himself between Victoria and the angry cowhand.

"Now, Deke, don't start nothing."

The other occupants of the place watched this with such attention it occurred to Victoria they wanted this cowboy to start something. In fact, some of them might come here for just such a spectacle.

Mercy, this was no place for Victoria Major, spinster. Heavens, no.

"Who's that?" Deke demanded of Mr. Callahan, waving his arm wildly at Victoria. "Where's Cyril?"

"You know Cyril got shot last week, in that rumpus

18

out front," Mr. Callahan replied in a placating tone.

"So you hired a—an old fuddy-duddy?"

Victoria stiffened in outrage.

"Ain't easy finding a piano player, Deke. It's her first night. Give her a chance, eh?"

"Well, God damn it." Deke, to Victoria's enormous relief, sat back down. "Tell 'er to play something lively. I'm here tryin' to enjoy myself."

Perhaps not the Chopin, then.

Mr. Callahan stepped over to the piano, a panicky look on his face. "Miss Major, you heard the man. Can you play something a little—well, livelier?"

"Certainly, Mr. Callahan." Her repertoire was large, including work of the best of Europe's composers. "Tchaikovsky, perhaps?"

Mr. Callahan looked blank, but didn't object to the suggestion.

Conversation had started back up in the room. Victoria drew upon her composure. She didn't want to get tossed out of this saloon on her first night. How humiliating would that be?

She crashed into the opening chords of Tchaikovsky's Piano Concerto Number One, putting all her energy into it. The saloon once more went silent, and heads craned so their owners could stare at her.

"Damn it!" Deke shouted.

Mr. Callahan came hurrying over again. "What in tarnation is that?"

"Fine music, Mr. Callahan."

"Well, the patrons don't like it much, and to be frank, neither do I. Don't you know any popular songs?"

"Certainly."

"Well, play 'em. And play 'em loud."

He stood there glaring at her, one eye twitching, as if waiting for her to begin. What would they consider a popular song, here in the West?

And could she remember any?

Back in the music halls she'd visited with Father, there had been artists who used the piano differently, to tinkle out simple tunes with considerable gusto. Perhaps, these residents of Wylder being simple folks, they required simple tunes also.

But for the life of her, she could recall only one or two.

She broke into "Mares Eat Oats," and Mr. Callahan visibly relaxed. So did the mood in the room.

He went back to the bar, and Victoria fought down the flush of humiliation while striving desperately to think of other such songs she might play.

For hours. Till the end of her stint here, when it was time to return to her lonely room at Hattie's.

****

Earl supposed he should go on home to his cabin up in the woods. It had begun to sink in that Wylder made no fit place for him these days. Especially with Eulalia Culpepper on the hunt.

The dream, all the while he'd been contemplating retirement, had been to get away off by himself. To avoid all the hustle and the string of constant problems needing his attention. He'd saved a bit while in the job of sheriff and could afford to just exist for a time.

Winter hibernation had seemed the perfect opportunity.

But now it came down to it—well, he was accustomed to the bustle. And that cabin felt pretty forlorn.

Maybe Sam was right and he needed a dog. But where did a man find a dog when he wanted one?

Last night he'd slept at the livery with his horse. He wouldn't be the first fellow to do so, and old Ulysses made decent company. Besides, the weather had turned so vile, only a fool would go riding up into them hills.

He'd leave tomorrow, as soon as the snow decided to settle down. Another night with Ulysses wouldn't hurt him.

Meanwhile, he could use a drink. Funny, how often that seemed to be the case lately. But hell, the whiskey dulled the ache in his knees, if not the one in his heart.

If he went into the Five Star Saloon or even the Long Horn, there would be folks there who would jump on him, want explanations as to why he was drinking his retirement away. They'd want conversation, and he wasn't in the mood for that—just whiskey. So he chose the Trail's End Saloon, despite the questionable atmosphere.

The place smelled bad inside, but he took a deep breath anyway, and felt some better. At least it was warm and full of life, even if it was—well, lowlife.

"Sheriff," Cody greeted him once again, as he stepped up to the bar.

"Didn't I tell you, boy? I ain't the sheriff no more."

Cody gave him an apologetic grin. "Right—no star on your shirt. At least you're still wearing your guns. The mood in here's ugly tonight. And Mr. Callahan's done up and left early. Whiskey?"

"Please."

Earl turned his head. The mood in the Trail's End

did, indeed, feel edgy. Too many people cooped up, like him, by the snow maybe.

"Don't want any bloodshed," Cody said as he put the whiskey in front of Earl. "Maybe you can still keep the peace."

"Not what I came for." Earl gave the room a cursory glance, using his lawman's senses, which after so many years differed very little from his ordinary ones. Gambling going on in the corner. Two men with one woman, at another table—that looked like trouble waiting to happen, all right. At a third table, a knot of cranky cowhands spoiling for a fight.

He sighed. Why had he come in here? Hadn't he had enough of smoothing rough waters?

Cody leaned toward him and said confidentially, "I think it's the piano player."

"Eh?" Earl looked at Cody in surprise. "Billy replaced Cyrus?" Cyrus, a young fellow, had got in the way of a stray bullet when an argument spilled over out front.

But to be sure, he could hear the tinkling of piano keys beneath the general racket. "Where'd he find another fellow to play?"

Cody rolled his eyes. "Ain't no fellow. It's a woman, and she's about to drive everyone insane."

Startled, Earl spun his gaze to the piano, which sat at an angle in one corner, half blocking the piano player from view. All he could see was a ruffled sleeve and the gleam of red hair.

Hmmm.

He strove to hear the music over the din. "A woman, eh? What's wrong with her? Can't she play?"

"She can. Sort of. But she only knows a couple of

songs and the fellas are getting right fed up with her. I think blood's gonna be spilled."

Earl narrowed his gaze. Hard to imagine anyone could even hear the music, or was bothering to listen. But as he well knew, music could affect the mood of a place and everybody in it.

That song she played now—sounded like a right dirge.

"Mercy," he breathed.

And just as he did, Deke Williams got up and faced the piano.

Deke, a cowhand from the Double L ranch, was well known as a troublemaker. The boy had a hair trigger and, in addition, liked his alcohol. He tended to go off on folks, and when he drank, things turned ugly. Fast.

Now he glared at the piano and shouted, "God damn it! Play something else, you ugly old hag, or I'll break all your fingers!"

Every nerve and sinew in Earl's body leaped to attention. This—this—was the sheriff's war cry, to which he'd never failed to respond. He had to remind himself, he was no longer sheriff.

He told Cody, from the corner of his mouth, "Send for Sheriff Wylder, quick now."

Cody bounced off. The room had fallen silent, and the figure behind the piano, whom Earl could still only glimpse, froze.

Ugly and old, was she? And a hag?

The fellas at the Trail's End, who came here for a good time, weren't likely to tolerate that. They liked their ladies young, or at least painted up to look young. And with a certain willingness of spirit.

He, Earl, had to get a better look at this woman.

"Now, Deke." He stepped up to the enraged cowhand. "That any way to talk to a lady?"

Deke turned to him. "That ain't no lady, Sheriff. She's—she's Satan's handmaiden."

Folk laughed, which broke the tension a little, though not enough to put Earl at ease.

"She's just playin' for us, ain't she?" he asked soothingly.

"She don't know but two songs in addition to those funeral tunes she's torturing that piano with. Why, Gus Wright would do better to hire her!" The town undertaker. "She's goin' to drive me plum mad."

"Sit down." Earl accompanied the command with pressure to Deke's shoulder. "I'll just have a word with her, all right? See if she can play something else."

Deke sat. His companions at the table eyed him with mingled amusement and commiseration.

Immediate trouble averted, Earl walked up to the piano. A female piano player—had Billy Callahan lost his mind? And an elderly hag, Deke said. Seemed like she'd do better playing hymns in church.

He cleared the side of the piano and halted, taking in the woman who sat at the keys in a straight-backed chair.

Not a hag, no, not by any stretch of the imagination, nor surely all that old. And most definitely a lady, dressed all prim-like in a dark blue traveling dress complete with hat. As foreign to this place as anyone could be, and looking frightened nearly out of her wits.

"Ma'am." He touched his hat.

"Sir," she returned, as if they'd just been

introduced at a cotillion or some such.

No, she wasn't young. Maybe in her forties, and now that he got a good look at her, he could see the lines at the corners of her eyes, and straining around her mouth. A life lived, as Earl well knew, left its marks on a person. Her eyes, though, were large and luminous— some pale color—and her hair... Oh, Lord, her hair! She wore it swept up beneath the ridiculous hat, and it gleamed like fire, seeming to ignite a responding fire in Earl's blood.

Damn it, he hadn't felt *that* in a while.

"Ma'am," he repeated, just for something to say. He wanted her engaged with him, focused on him. Interested. He wanted her attention in a way he couldn't hope to explain.

"Seems there've been some complaints about your choice of music."

"Yes." Her lips trembled when she spoke, which called forth yet another unexpected response from the region of Earl's heart. "I've done my best. But quite clearly, that's not good enough. Perhaps I should leave."

Chapter Five

The man who had walked up to Victoria's piano brought a feeling of safety with him—of reassurance. She already thought of it as her piano, even after only a few hours, because the two of them had suffered together. And its high back partially screened her from the room.

Now she inspected this man in front of her and wondered who he was. Not a young man, by any means, he wore a battered hat and had a gun strapped to his side. A heavy coat covered bulky shoulders, a strong figure of just above average height. His hair, gone to silver, matched a pair of lengthy sideburns and a fine moustache. He had a weathered face and some of the bluest eyes she'd ever seen.

"Well, now." He placed an elbow on top of the piano and leaned, effectively screening her from the room and affording a few minutes of blessed relief. "That would be a shame—you leavin', I mean."

"It would not. They hate my playing." She gathered up a raft of music sheets in front of her. "That has been made abundantly clear. I'd better just admit it and…and slink away like a kicked dog."

He cocked his head. "You the kind of woman who gives up easy?" The bright blue gaze slid over her face. "Got to admit, you don't look it."

"This stint has been anything but easy, Mr.—"

"Hanson. Earl Hanson." He stuck out his hand. "And you are—?"

"Victoria Major." She had no choice but to slip her fingers into his hand, which felt broad and horny. She wondered if he'd heard that cowhand call her a hag. The second time that had happened in the past five days. Then she wondered why she cared what he'd heard.

Just another man in this accursed town. Did it matter what Earl Hanson thought of her?

"Missus Major—"

"Miss. It's Miss Major." She glared into his eyes. "I'm a spinster."

"Ah. I thought—"

"People frequently do assume I must be a widow, because of my age."

He didn't look shocked at her direct statement. In fact, his expression didn't change. He asked, "What seems to be the problem with the piano playing?"

"I have no idea, quite frankly."

"That fella there says you only know two songs."

"I am, sir, a classically trained pianist. I know hundreds of songs. But not what they wish to hear."

"Ah."

"Earlier on in the evening, Mr. Callahan said to play something lively, so I assayed with a bold Tchaikovsky piece. I also tried Beethoven and Handel."

"I think Mr. Callahan might have meant you should play songs these folks know."

"I understand that." Victoria's face heated. "I don't know what they know. I did play *Mares Eat Oats* and *Sidewalks of New York* until I thought they would begin throwing things at me. They're even averse to Stephen

Foster."

"Lots of folks here fought in the War Between the States—or fled it. Mr. Foster's music might make 'em feel a bit tetchy."

"From what I can see, Mr. Hanson, everything makes them feel tetchy."

"An astute observation. Listen, Miss Major, there must be some other songs you can play. How about 'Buffalo Gals'?"

"I beg your pardon?"

He whistled a tune. He made an excellent job of it, right on key, but Victoria didn't recognize the song and shook her head.

" 'My Darling Clementine'?"

"I'm afraid not."

"Oh my darlin', oh my darlin'—" He sang well too, in a resonant baritone.

She wagged her head again.

" 'Yellow Rose of Texas'?"

She might not mind listening to him sing for the rest of the evening, but she suspected he'd tire of it all too soon.

"Well, play me the two you do know."

"I'm afraid if I play them again, there will be violence. It's why I tried playing the Liszt. I don't dare play Chopin again."

He gave her a blank, blue stare. "Just play 'em."

Hastily, she gave him abbreviated versions of "Mares Eat Oats"—to an outcry from the room—and "Sidewalks of New York." He stood like a bulwark between her and the rowdy room all the while.

"Miss Major, you play very well."

"Thank you."

"But you might put a bit more life in it. Some flourishes. Here, shove over."

"I beg your pardon?"

"Let me have the chair."

She arose, feeling stiff and rusty, and he took her place. He stretched his gnarled fingers above the yellowed keys and seemed to gather himself before he started to play.

The old piano sang. It chortled, it chuckled. Suddenly, its out-of-tune jangle worked in its favor rather than the opposite.

A dull cheer rose from the room at large.

He finished the tune, though not without errors. It didn't matter. His music had life. It possessed energy.

"There. My fingers aren't as nimble as they used to be."

"Where did you learn to play like that?"

"Like that? In places like this, long ago. I originally learned to play piano at church—believe it or not."

"That piece you played is the same one you whistled, right?"

"Yeah, that was 'Buffalo Gals.' Think you can pick it up?"

Victoria hesitated. She inspected him from the battered hat downward, her gaze lingering on those luxurious sideburns and the flowing moustache. She wanted to say, "If you'll teach me," but didn't quite dare. So she merely inclined her head.

"I'm sure I can."

"You can repeat the songs you play throughout the evening, but you have to have a bag of them." He got up and ushered her back into the chair. "You try it. I'll stand guard."

Victoria smiled. "That's very kind of you."

"Don't think I've ever been described as kind. But I don't appreciate trouble none."

She picked out the tune he'd played on the yellowed keys, then added a few chords. It lacked the raucous jangle he'd given it. But she heard no complaints from the room.

Rather than standing guard, Mr. Hanson pulled up a chair from one of the tables and sat nearby, arms crossed and his pistol very much in evidence.

For the first time since Victoria had come to Wylder, she felt safe.

Chapter Six

The tune went through Victoria's head later, when she lay in her bed at the Morgans' house, trying to sleep, replete with the words Earl Hanson had murmured not quite under his breath while sitting beside her.

Buffalo gals won't you come out tonight, come out tonight, come out tonight...and dance by the light of the moon?

Victoria had no doubt as to what sort of women these Buffalo gals might be. They probably dressed in bright pink gowns that displayed a wealth of bosom, and they liked to dance. Definitely not aging hags.

She hated to admit how much the slur—*hag*—hurled by an ignorant stranger—had hurt. She'd never been a vain woman, never had much reason to be vain. Most suitors, when she was young, liked a girl with more curves than she possessed, less bookish. Many had an aversion to red hair.

But now, at the age of nearly forty-eight, it seemed the term "hag" had come home to roost. She'd run out of chances, and her heart—once so wild beneath her ladylike exterior—realized it had to give up on dreams of love.

Those were for other people, or for the girl she'd once been. Yes, she'd dreamed of love and marriage. Neither had come along, and she'd learned survival instead. A measure of joy in her music.

That was what had made the scandal back in St. Louis so surprising. She thought she'd surrendered all vulnerability. Her heart, it seemed, had held on to some.

Now the best she could hope for would be learning a rash of new songs to keep the wild folk penned up in the Trail's End Saloon happy.

She wondered whether Earl Hanson would turn up again. He'd sat beside her quite patiently most of the night, tipping back on the rear legs of the chair, and then had disappeared, seemingly into thin air, when the place shut down.

No one had bothered her, with him nearby. He'd even nodded when she assayed some Strauss waltzes, as if he enjoyed them.

Would he be back? She hoped so.

In the morning, when she went down to breakfast, Hattie gave her a doubtful look.

"How was the saloon last night?"

Victoria considered the question. The word *dreadful* came readily to her lips. But it hadn't been, not all of it.

She slid into a seat at the table and accepted the cup of tea Hattie offered. "At first I thought they were going to take my head off. Or start throwing things. Then—do you know a man called Earl Hanson?"

Hattie looked surprised. "The sheriff?"

"He's the sheriff?" No wonder he carried that air of protective authority.

"Well, no, not any more. Though he was, for years. Retired now, I think."

Victoria thought of the flowing, silver hair. "I see."

"Funny thing—Earl Hanson being in the Trail's

End Saloon. He rarely drinks. And he never set foot in there, far as I know, unless he was hauling somebody off to jail."

"He sat near me and kept the rowdies at bay."

"That sounds like him."

"Is he—married?"

Hattie gave her a sharp glance. "No. Never has been, to my knowledge. It takes a strong woman to want a lawman for husband. I don't think I could endure it. Why? You interested?"

"Me? Don't be silly. I'm a spinster through and through. Just—he seemed very kind."

"Kind? Earl Hanson? Don't believe that's the word I'd use to describe him. Most folks say he's hard as nails."

"Hmm. He taught me a song—'Buffalo Gals.' "

"Ha! Earl Hanson did?" Hattie chortled over it.

"Yes." Victoria raised defiant eyes to her friend's face. "Quite frankly, I'm hoping he'll teach me some more."

"Victoria Major!"

Victoria flushed. "I didn't mean it that way. It's just—if I don't learn the kinds of songs the patrons of the Trail's End Saloon want to hear, there's going to be a riot."

Hattie propped her hands on her hips. "I still say you need to find work elsewhere. That's no place for you."

"I guess I'm stubborn. I don't want to give in and let them chase me out."

"Well, I admire a woman with backbone. Just don't be foolish about it, hear?"

"I hear you," Victoria agreed.

****

She arrived at the saloon early that afternoon, while the place was still quiet. Cody, the barman, rolled his eyes at her like a spooked horse.

"What are you doing here? You're not due for hours yet."

Victoria could scarcely believe it either. "I thought I'd get some practice in, try to learn the songs your customers like to hear." She wrinkled her nose involuntarily. The place might be empty, but it still smelled bad. Did they never clean in here?

"Uh—" Cody ran his gaze over her. "Just a suggestion, but it might help your popularity a whit if you dressed a little more—" He paused, apparently lacking the words.

"Colorfully?" Victoria supplied, thinking of Mr. Callahan.

"I was gonna say a bit—er—looser," Cody admitted.

Victoria stiffened. She possessed but the two decent gowns, both suitable for traveling or teaching, and staid in the extreme. "No, you may not suggest I should dress like a loose woman."

To her surprise, Cody grinned. "Want a drink? That might help. And Mr. Callahan always allowed Cyrus three drinks a night."

"No, I do not want a drink." To encourage her to loosen her morals, no doubt.

She set her folio of music sheets on the bar. "Tell me, has Mr. Hanson been in?"

"Earl? Not today. Somebody saw him heading out of town on that big brown horse of his. Probably headed back up to his cabin."

"Oh." Victoria strove mightily to discipline her disappointment. What more had she expected? "He has a cabin outside town?"

"Yup. In the hills west of here."

So—no comforting presence parked next to Victoria this evening. How would she endure it?

She sighed deeply and retreated to her piano.

****

Earl sighted the cabin through the trees, and waited for his heart to rise. For years he'd dreamed of having this place, a haven where he could retreat from the deadly pace of the sheriff's life. He'd wanted, on some level, to return to his past.

His father had been a doctor, first back East and then in various small towns before settling in Wylder. The job had kept his family comfortable enough, but there'd always been a wild spark in Earl's heart that made him reach for something beyond the limits of any town. Being the oldest son, he'd been expected to be reliable, a good example to the others. He could still remember his mother harping on about it.

But at the age of eighteen, he'd packed up his things and struck out for the wilder life, and had ended up in a cabin not unlike this one, in company with the only woman he'd ever been able to call wife.

Funny, he reflected now, how it had all come full circle—how his mother's words had stuck and he'd become dependable after all, with a whole town full of folks relying on him, as sheriff in Wylder.

And, another cabin. He'd felled the trees to build it himself—not too old for that, yet—and built it too, with some help from friends. It was meant to be his reward. But—

Nah, his heart didn't rise when he saw it now, despite the beauty of the spot he'd selected. All those tall pines sheltering the place, and a fine view out over the valley.

He knew it would be cold inside. Cold and empty. Certainly not the comforting nest he'd envisioned.

He dismounted in the front yard and led Ulysses round to the lean-to on the sheltered side. Taking his time over it, he settled the horse in with clean straw and good winter feed. Only then did he enter the cabin.

Just as he'd thought. The fire long out, the cabin's interior felt colder than the air outside. He'd do better to bed down with Ulysses, as he had the past several nights, than crawl into that bed over against the wall.

He gave a shiver and left his heavy coat on while he got the fire going. Was he turning soft, or what? Back in that other cabin, when they lived together, tending the fire had been Little Bird's sacred duty, and he could still hear her calling to him in her broken English, "Husband, bring me more kindling. Fill the wood box for me."

He'd been happy to do that. His body, young and strong, had delighted in wielding the axe, in providing for his woman and the child to come. Now he could almost see her, in the movements of his own hands.

Gone. She was gone now, like everyone else from his past. One of the disadvantages, he supposed, of living a long life. It had been thirty-five years since he'd been with Little Bird. How could he feel her here in this room so strongly?

He was getting spooked, that was what, up here alone. Next thing he knew, he'd be seeing her ghost. And if that happened, well…

Then the guilt would come. 'Cause he'd promised himself long ago if he ever had a woman, he'd make sure her life was better for being with him.

Only…he hadn't.

Enough of all this. He was a practical man, wasn't he? And long past the age for—well, longings.

With the fire burning well and taking the dead chill out of the room, he walked to the corner and unearthed a battered old guitar.

This was what he'd come for. He'd spend the night here, give Ulysses a chance to rest, and then take his old six-string back to town.

As foolish an impulse as that might be.

Chapter Seven

"It was a disaster," Victoria admitted to Hattie over tea the following morning. "An unmitigated disaster. I played the very few songs I'd practiced over and over again until those men began to shout at me. Then— forgive the phrase—all hell broke loose. Some of them walked out. Some just turned—well, ugly. At least three fights erupted."

One, she felt sure, had been prompted by her playing, or lack thereof. At last Mr. Callahan, who'd been there on the premises, had come over and told her to leave early. Her cheeks still burned with humiliation over that.

Father had never been asked to leave a venue. Nor had she, when with him. But that hadn't been Wylder, Wyoming or the Trail's End Saloon, which she began to perceive was a small sampling of Hell.

She could scarcely believe what a difference Earl Hanson's presence made. How many times last night had she wished he sat beside her, balancing on the rear legs of his chair?

"No matter," Hattie said comfortingly. "It's over now."

"Is it?"

"You certainly won't be going back there again."

Victoria stiffened where she sat. Never would she have suspected she had a stubborn streak—she'd always cooperated with Father, all his choices and instructions. But she found the notion of quitting her job at the Trail's End as distressing as continuing to work it—or, nearly.

She fastened her gaze on Hattie. "I haven't even been paid yet."

"No, Victoria—"

"I'll be darned if I'll walk out before that man pays me for all the suffering I've endured."

"If you're worried about paying us for your room, don't be. I'll have a word with Tom."

Victoria knew Tom hadn't been as enthusiastic as Hattie about letting her room here. The prospect of her paying board had sweetened the pot.

She lifted her chin. "I'm planning on going in early again today, to practice. Surely you must know some other songs I might learn."

Hattie sang while Victoria helped her do up the breakfast dishes. Her head teeming with lyrics and tunes, she at last went up to her room.

There, she took a hard look at herself in the speckled mirror. No one had called her a hag last night. She supposed she must count that as an improvement. Though she was pretty sure she'd caught the term *that old bat* when complaints about her music flew.

Earnestly, she stared into her own eyes. Was she an old bat? She supposed she did appear old to those cowhands, most still in their first flush of youth. They didn't know that inside she remained the young girl she'd once been.

She pressed her hands to her chest to alleviate the pain. She had no way to alter her appearance—no other clothing to wear. Not a great deal of bosom to display, even if she chose to stoop to that. She was a decent woman, wasn't she? And comported herself as such.

But maybe she could rearrange her hair, just a bit…

****

The first thing Earl saw when he stepped into the Trail's End later that afternoon, was Miss Victoria Major. A rush of warmth came over him—caused, no doubt, by coming in out of the cold.

He'd taken his time settling Ulysses at the livery, telling himself there was no hurry. But he couldn't deny, now, a little tingle of anticipation.

"Sheriff!" someone called.

"I ain't the sheriff no more," he called back, sounding grumpier than he intended, and Victoria's head jerked up. Her pale eyes fixed on him.

She looked different this afternoon. It certainly couldn't be attributed to her dress—the same he'd seen her wearing last time. Or her slightly haunted expression. Her hair—that was it. Before, she'd had it all swept up in the back, under that hat. Now the hat had disappeared, and she wore part of her hair down over one shoulder. Red as flame.

Earl's toes began to tingle. Yeah, that was the warmth returning to them.

"Sheriff," Cody called, "want a drink?"

Earl sighed. "Not just yet." A bit early for whiskey, though he didn't doubt a stiff one might benefit him at the moment.

How should he go about this? It had been a long time since he'd approached a lady.

Which Miss Victoria Major was, quite unmistakably.

He pinned a smile on his face and headed over to the piano where she sat. She popped up on her feet when he reached her, like a gopher.

"Mr. Hanson."

"Miss Major. I have to say, I'm right surprised to see you here, still."

She made a little face that pursed her lips and put doubt in her eyes. "Last night did not go particularly well. In fact, I was asked to leave early."

"You were, eh?"

"I think they grew weary of the same few songs. And, well, even when I play 'Buffalo Gals' it comes out sounding more like an étude than a—well, jangle."

"They like the jangle in here, and that's a fact. I may have a solution." Earl swung the guitar off his back, and her eyes widened. He took off his coat too, and drew up a chair next to hers.

"What's that?"

"A guitar." Hadn't she ever seen one before? And her an educated woman.

"Well, yes, I see that. But—you play?"

"Used to. Fingers ain't as spry as they once were. But I reckon I can play you some tunes, and you can pound 'em out alongside of me. Beats whistling."

Victoria's eyes promptly filled with tears. Earl stared in horror as a couple of them spilled over and trickled down her cheeks.

"Here, now—"

"You'd do that for me?"

"Well—"

"I thought you'd left town. They said you'd left town."

"I did. Rode up to my cabin to fetch Louise, here.

Stayed overnight."

"Louise?"

"The guitar. Spent a lot o' time alone with her. Had to give her a woman's name." Earl directed a cursory glance at the instrument. "She ain't much to look at any more, but, well, looks ain't everything."

Miss Victoria pawed at the tears on her cheeks. "Of course not."

"She still sounds pretty sweet. Here, sit down." Folks in the bar were staring, not that they numbered many, this early in the day.

She sat with a little bump that must have rattled her teeth. Her pale gaze still clung to Earl. "This is so very nice of you. Considerate."

"Well, now, Miss Vicky." How long had it been since a woman looked at him that way? "One word most folks here in Wylder won't use to describe me is 'nice.' "

"I must beg to differ with them."

Dropping his gaze from hers, Earl tuned the guitar. It took a bit of doing, after that cold ride.

Surely it was just gratitude he saw shining in her eyes. She'd had a rough go, had Miss Vicky.

He played a little tune when he got Louise where he wanted her, just to test things out.

Victoria smiled. He wasn't sure he'd seen her smile before—at least not genuine, like that.

"I like that tune. What's it called?"

Earl struggled to remember. He had a lot of songs floating around in his head, and remembered names of only a few of them.

" 'Roll, Alabama,' I think."

"You're self-taught?"

"I am. And nowhere near up to your caliber. But it will serve."

"Please play that one again."

He did, and she listened—really listened, with her head tilted to one side and her eyes fixed on nothing. Then, damned if she didn't play the tune with her fingers—just let it flow out over the keys.

This was a woman with some talent. But she was right, it came out sounding like some highfalutin concert.

"That's good, real good," he encouraged.

She lit up again. "You think so? Will they—the customers—like that one?"

"Don't you worry about them cowboys just now. Think about the music." He wanted to keep that look on her face, the light in her eyes. "Now play it again, only toss in some extra notes—like this." He played the tune once more, only fancier. "Let's play it together."

They did, and when they finished applause broke out in the room. Miss Victoria flushed rosy pink.

Billy Callahan came walking over. "What are you up to, Earl? This a duet now?"

"Nay, Billy. Just showing your piano player some tricks."

"An act of mercy, is it? Or are you gonna expect to be paid?"

"I wouldn't turn down a glass of whiskey."

"You're welcome to my allotment," Miss Victoria said. "I'm allowed three drinks a night and never take them."

Earl shot her a look before telling Billy, "Bring me a whiskey, and the lady a beer."

"Beer? Me? I never drink beer."

"If you want to work here, you better start." Maybe it would relax her enough so she'd enjoy the playing.

"Let's try that one again."

It felt good moving his fingers over the strings, trying to keep up with her when she got going. Cody brought the drinks and set them on the piano. Victoria eyed hers in a manner which said, *It's there, but I don't have to drink it.*

Earl took a gulp of his. It eased the ache in his knees, ruined by too many years in the saddle.

She asked, "Do you know 'Yellow Rose of Texas'?"

"Sure do."

Time went away—Earl couldn't remember when last that had happened for him, either—and more people filtered in. Earl thought about leaving, but he suspected that Miss Victoria—at last—was having a good time. She'd even taken a sip or two of the beer, though she made a face afterwards.

At last he moved to put Louise aside.

"Please, don't leave." She reached out with those graceful hands of hers and caught his arm. Flat-out touched him.

"But the regulars are in the house. They don't want to hear me."

"I'm not sure they want to hear me either. I think we sound nice together."

They did. The old guitar and the out-of-tune piano played very well in harmony. "All right," he said, against his better judgment.

Earl felt it when Victoria began to relax. During their first break she gulped down half her beer. After that, she pounded the keys harder and even threw in a few trills and runs.

The patrons in the saloon seemed content with it. At least, no one shouted or threw things. A few came by to clasp Earl on the shoulder and greet him.

"Sheriff."

Victoria's cheeks acquired a bit of a flush, and the hair trailing over her shoulder kind of flared out whenever she leaned toward Earl. He took to speaking to her when he had the chance, just for the effect.

"You want another one o' those?" he tapped her beer glass.

She blinked at it in surprise. "I drank that?"

"Sure did." He signaled Cory for another beer and a second whiskey. Hang, if she was over her limit.

She fanned herself. "I am very thirsty. I don't remember it being so warm in here before."

"Heats up some, as the evening moves along."

"Tell me, why do they call you 'Sheriff'—I mean, I understand you used to be the sheriff, correct?" Absent-mindedly, she tossed back the dregs of her beer. "But you're re-retired."

"Takes a while for folks to get it out of their head, after so many years."

"How long were you sheriff?"

"About eight years here, and over to Scobey before that, in Big Sky country." He'd taken his first job sheriffing back when Miss Victoria would have been a girl. He wondered how she would have looked then. Tall. Slender. Well, she was still both. And with all that red hair.

He leaned toward her just for the sake of it. "Let's play 'Old Dan Tucker.' "

They played till closing, when Earl stood up,

feeling stiff, and turned to her. "Well, Miss Victoria, looks like you had yourself a successful evening."

"Only because you were here." She reached out to him again, her hand clasping his. "How can I thank you?"

"No need, Miss Vicky. I had a good time."

"So did I."

She smiled at him, and he grinned back at her. They stood there that way several minutes, him grinning like an idiot and her holding onto his hand.

"Why don't you let me see you home?" he heard himself ask.

"Why, it's not far. Just to the Morgans'. But I'd appreciate that."

She gathered up her sheet music, none of which she'd used, and closed the lid over the piano keys, like it was a valuable instrument.

He slung Louise over his shoulder, and they set out, watched by Cody and a few regulars.

Outside, the wind caught them, and Earl smelled snow in the offing.

"Another storm comin'," he remarked. It had been a bad year already, and the year wasn't very old.

The wind buffeted Victoria, and she seized hold of Earl's arm. Only to steady herself, he supposed. But it felt—

Good.

"I suppose you'll be heading back to your cabin, to beat the storm, I mean."

"I probably should." Though the thought of getting snowed in there alone held little appeal.

"I'm just here." They paused in front of the Morgans' house, and she turned to face him. "Really,

Mr. Hanson, I cannot thank you enough—"

"We'll have to do it again."

"I'd like that. I'm sure there are many more songs for you to impart."

"No doubt."

"Plus, your presence does seem to keep the rowdies at bay."

"Well, now. Maybe I should stay and weather the storm here in town."

"That way we could practice together again." Did those pale eyes of hers brighten? "If you wanted to, that is."

"I'd be pleased to."

"Well, I'd best go in."

To Earl's surprise—no, make that astonishment—he entertained an impulse to kiss her. He absolutely couldn't follow through on it. Instead, to his even greater astonishment, he lifted her hand to his lips.

He didn't actually kiss her fingers, but it was meant.

What the hell, he wondered as she slipped into the house, had got into him?

Chapter Nine

The storm, just another of those that visited throughout the season, came with icy winds that shrieked out of the west, rushing down Wylder Street the way Eulalia Culpepper did. Earl, lying snug inside Ulysses' stall at the livery, decided it wasn't the worst place to be.

He'd built his cabin strong, sure to keep him warm. But a house, like any other place, needed life inside it on a regular basis. He'd have to make up his mind to hunker down there and turn it into something more than a cold box built of logs, or give it up as a bad bet.

One thing was certain, he thought as he arose. Sleeping on the floor, even with a thick layer of straw beneath him, did his old bones no good. He groaned, and Ulysses gave an interested stare.

"Thanks, old soul, for not stepping on me while I was asleep." He patted the big horse, knowing Ulysses would never do that. They'd traveled far too many miles together, and relied on each other too heavily.

He hobbled out to the main area of the livery, his knees giving him the very devil, and peered outside. Half a foot of snow already covered the ground, much of it blown into drifts and peaks.

"Well, damn." He wouldn't be going far today.

The Trail's End Saloon wasn't far.

Now, why had that thought stolen into his head?

He'd set Miss Victoria up proper—she now knew a number of songs. And Billy Callahan hadn't hired him to play his guitar.

He needn't go back there tonight. Or ever again.

That thought made him feel uneasy, kind of prickly all over, like he had fever. But he didn't much like the way Miss Victoria made him feel, either. At least—well, he liked it. But he had no business entertaining such feelings. Not at his time of life. Anyway, the poor woman wouldn't welcome such attentions from him—an old, used-up trapper-turned-sheriff, turned—

What the hell was he now?

A sigh stole from him, and he turned away from the view between the livery's big double doors.

Miss Victoria was a respectable woman, a spinster, for God's sake. She'd found herself in a bit of difficulty—in the wrong place, he had to say—and he'd helped her out. That made an end to it. No reason to wake up in the middle of the night, thinking of her. Or wondering how she'd look with all that red hair loose, hanging around her shoulders.

"Ya old fool," he muttered under his breath. "Thought you gave up such ideas long ago."

****

Victoria woke with a moan and mustered enough strength to lift a hand to her head. Her room lay quiet, and she could hear snowflakes hitting the lone window, icy tapping of the pellets on the thick glass. What time was it? Her room lay quiet, but the rest of the house did not.

She could hear Hattie hurrying about below, her voice and those of the children. She, Victoria, had slept in. Of course, it had been very late when she and Earl left the saloon.

Earl.

The thought of him shot through her like one of those rockets on the fourth of July, and caused her to sit up in the bed. Pain, like that from a descending axe, promptly split her head.

How much of that beer had she drunk last night? Not above a glass and a half. Nasty stuff it was, with a bitter, grainy taste. In the past, the most she'd ever taken was a genteel glass of sherry. But she got thirsty playing piano for hours, and the beer had served to quench that thirst.

Ah, but there were consequences, she thought as she staggered to the window. In life, there always were. In fact, it seemed she could trace the course of her life by the choices she'd made and what came of them.

Nothing good.

She tried to peer through the window, and failed. Big white blotches adhered to the glass and obscured her view.

She'd always been poor at looking ahead. Though she appeared staid and straight-laced, she tended to jump at things. And her heart…

Well, her heart had got her into trouble a few times, and refused to learn its lessons.

Once, she'd believed in letting her heart make choices. She'd listened to it, even when it whispered wild things. Like, true love would one day find her. Ha! That notion had caused her to turn down the one good man who ever offered for her.

Roger Trent. She remembered him fondly, even now. A respectable man—she'd liked him well enough. But she hadn't loved him, just as he hadn't loved her.

She'd gone so far as to tell him so.

"Perhaps love will grow between us, Victoria," he'd suggested. But she hadn't believed in that, not hard enough.

And now she found herself here at the age of nearly forty-eight—alone. How had that happened? No home, no family of her own—which, at least, she'd surely have had with Roger. And because of a scandal, fleeing the job around which her life, such as it was, had revolved.

Her head pounded harder, and for a moment her insides heaved alarmingly. She fought the sickness down, put on her wrapper, and tiptoed down to the kitchen.

"There's no school today," Hattie greeted her. "Too much snow. I'm trying to keep the children occupied with chores." She took a second look at Victoria. "You don't look very well today. Are you all right?"

"I have a headache fit to knock me down." Victoria sank into a chair at the table, wishing the children might be just a bit quieter.

"Let me get you a powder." Over her shoulder, Hattie asked, "How did last evening go?"

"It went—well." Victoria thought it over as best she could. The music that seemed to flow so much better when the piano and guitar played together. Earl Hanson's comfortable presence, keeping the rowdies at bay. There'd been a few moments when she'd almost—almost enjoyed herself.

"Just a couple more evenings and I'll get paid," she told Hattie, as if that alone concerned her. "Then I can give you what I owe."

"I told you not to worry about that."

"I'm sure Tom would like to receive the board I promised."

Hattie set a cup in front of Victoria. "Drink up, if you want to work tonight."

Did she? Well, perhaps so.

****

Hours later, the Trail's End Saloon looked conspicuously empty. From Victoria's place behind the piano, she could see that barely half the tables were occupied, and floor space abounded.

She realized that, ordinarily, many of the regular patrons must be cowhands in off the outlying ranches. Given the storm, they hadn't ridden in.

Would Earl Hanson show? No sign of him yet. Victoria fussed with her sheet music, which she rarely used and suspected she kept around just for reassurance, and thought about it.

With pickings so slim, maybe she wouldn't be needed to play this evening. She motioned to Cody behind the bar and when he stepped over asked, "It's pretty quiet in here. Will Mr. Callahan want me tonight?"

Cody shrugged. "He hasn't come in."

"What do you think I should do?"

"I'd play, if I were you. The folks who are here will want some entertainment. Would you like a beer?"

Victoria's stomach promptly revolted, and her head gave a sympathetic pang. But she said, "Yes, please."

"I'll bring it right over. You expecting Earl tonight?"

Expecting? No. hoping—that was a different matter.

Yet he didn't turn up among the establishment's sparse attendees. Victoria played softly. She gave them "Yellow Rose of Texas," "Clementine," and even snuck in a Strauss waltz, which they seemed to enjoy.

Maybe she could educate them, eventually, on finer music. If she stayed, that was.

She was playing "Sidewalks of New York" when the wing doors flew open and Earl blew in. He had his hat pulled well down against the wind, and Louise on his back.

Victoria tried to contain her gladness, but it slipped out, causing her to fumble the keys. She didn't want to admit how much she'd wanted to see him, or how happy his appearance made her feel. She didn't want to acknowledge she'd done her hair just for him tonight, leaving not one but three curls down.

But oh, was she glad to see him!

Maybe he'd just come for a drink, she thought, tamping down her euphoria. But then why had he brought Louise?

He cast one look around the room before coming directly to her. She'd left his chair from last night in place, and he set Louise on it, produced a cloth, and dried her off most carefully.

Battered and old she might be, but he clearly valued her anyway.

"Good evening," Victoria told him. "I wasn't sure you meant to come."

"No," he returned, leaving her to wonder just what that meant. He eyed her slowly where she sat, his gaze lingering a bit too long on her hair.

"It's quiet in here tonight."

"That ain't a bad thing."

She waved a hand in invitation. "Join me?"

"Sure thing, Miss Vicky. Just let me get outside a whiskey first. Plum cold out there."

She watched him leaning on the bar, speaking to Cody. When he turned back, he gave her the smile that twitched the luxurious moustache of his, and she felt herself light from within.

How would that moustache feel if he kissed her?

Lord have mercy, she had no business thinking such things. Best to concentrate on the music.

And on the warm, comfortable feeling that filled her inside.

Chapter Ten

They sang. That evening, while the wind blew outside and only a handful of people patronized the Trail's End Saloon, they did.

Earl started it, humming along to one of the songs as he strummed in time with Victoria's playing, and then adding the words in his rich baritone.

When Victoria's heart rose, she joined in. She didn't have what Father had called a *voice*, but she didn't do so badly and loved harmony. She added the harmony now, to Earl's rumble, and it sounded good.

When they finished, the patrons in the saloon applauded. Applauded. Half the time, she felt convinced they weren't even listening.

She and Earl grinned at one another.

" 'Yellow Rose'?" he suggested.

They launched into it, and a few of the patrons joined in. Before she knew it, they had a sing-along going.

"Play 'Shenandoah,' " someone called out, and Earl said, "Well, now, don't know as Miss Vicky's familiar with that one." He sang it, and a few other voices joined him. Gamely, Victoria played accompaniment.

The mood in the place had changed. Cody leaned on the bar, and folks swayed in their seats. For the first time since she'd come here, Victoria felt as if she might be among friends.

When the evening ended, Earl said, "I'll see you home."

Her heart bounded, but she said, "No need."

"Of course I will. It's still blowin' out."

"All right."

Snow covered the wooden planks of the sidewalk and made walking difficult. Victoria told herself that was the only reason she took Earl's arm.

"Terrible weather," she remarked, silently glad of it.

"About to blow itself out. It'll be clear tomorrow."

"Will you—um—return to your cabin then?"

"Haven't quite made up my mind."

"I enjoyed myself tonight."

"Me too."

In front of the Morgans' door, she slipped and nearly fell. Both of Earl's arms came around her. Facing him, she gazed into his eyes. "Will you be back at the Trail's End tomorrow evening?"

"Well, now, I guess that depends." He stirred his feet uneasily. "Seems you're doing fine on your own. Don't need me none."

She did. *She did.*

"Besides, Cody was telling me, when I went in there tonight, folks is already starting to talk about us."

"Talk?"

"Linking our names, like. I wouldn't want to besmirch your reputation."

Didn't want his name linked with hers, more like. "Oh."

He stood awkwardly silent.

"I understand," she said at last. "You've been very

56

good to me, so patient, teaching me your songs—"

"I enjoyed it, Miss Vicky. You're a fine musician, much better than I'll ever be. I'd like to hear, sometime, how you ended up in Wylder, Wyoming, instead of playin' in some grand concert hall."

"Someday, I'd like to tell you."

He released her elbows. "You'd best go in now, out of the cold."

"Yes." She wanted to say a hundred other things— beg him to send her word if he decided to ride out of town. Ask him to stay one more day, one more evening…she dared voice none of it.

He wished to avoid scandal, and scandal was a terrible thing. How could she mistake that, when it was the very reason she'd come here in the first place?

"Tell you what," he said, just as if she had asked. "I'll stop by here tomorrow and let you know, if the weather clears and I decide to leave for the cabin."

She studied his eyes. "Won't that make folks talk?"

He shrugged.

Her heart bounded. "I'd appreciate that."

He gave a decisive nod. "Good night, then, Miss Vicky." He crammed his hat tighter on his head and disappeared into the darkness.

****

The weather cleared miraculously the next morning, just as Earl had predicted. He told himself he really needed to go on up to the cabin, lose himself there, and fulfill the promise he'd made when he retired. A measure of seclusion. Time to himself after being buffeted by the waves of Wylder's fortunes for so long.

By morning, he'd become convinced of it. The

blue skies and hills all covered in white beckoned him.

Other things served to persuade him also, including the fact that, no matter how he tried, he couldn't stop thinking about Miss Vicky. How sweet her lips looked when she sang. The confiding way she leaned toward him when they made harmony. The way her eyes lit with interest when he spoke to her.

He couldn't be developing feelings for Miss Vicky. Well, he certainly could. A rare type of woman she was, smart and talented, and with a sense of humor buried beneath all that propriety.

And yes, the propriety bothered him. He couldn't let himself grow feelings for a woman like that, because she'd expect things, commitments he no longer believed he could make.

She deserved those commitments. But not from him, not at this point in his life.

Maybe he needed to stop by the Wylder County Social Club and work out a few kinks. He'd been there in the past, though not recently because people tended to talk. Curiously, he could never clearly remember the services he got there.

Damn people and their talk, anyway.

Late that next morning, with the sun shining and a feeling of restlessness riding him, he saddled up Ulysses, hung Louise from his saddle, and headed on over to the Morgans' place.

Following the storm, folks were out and about—lots of folks. Women headed to the mercantile with shopping baskets. The bank looked to be hopping, and cowhands had come in from the outlying ranches, sent on errands, no doubt.

He turned his eyes toward the jail. It would be the

most natural thing to walk in there, but it was another man's place now.

"I ain't sheriff no more," he muttered, and traveled to the Morgans' door.

"Sheriff Hanson? I am so glad I caught you."

He froze in place, a feeling of dread settling over him. *Caught* seemed to be the apt word. Because he'd know that voice anywhere.

"Mrs. Culpepper." He turned and touched the brim of his hat.

She steamed up just like one of those boats he used to see trundling along on the Mississippi, her eyes fixed on him in a way that argued no escape. She wore her coat with the poor little fox trapped around her neck, and an oversized hat that nevertheless failed to completely hide her helmet of hair.

She simpered at him. "I've asked you to call me Eulalia."

And I've asked you not to call me "Sheriff." Or follow along behind me like some fish wife.

As if.

He tore his gaze from that of the poor fox. Even when he'd done some trapping, long ago, he'd avoided causing the critters undue pain, or treating them to this poor animal's fate.

"What can I do for you, Miss Eulalia?"

"Well, now." She attempted to look arch, a procedure so distressing it tightened Earl's balls in fear. "I'm pleased you asked. There's a supper at the church this Sunday. They're looking to raise the funds for a new roof, and so, you see, it's for a good cause and benefits Wylder. I know you always concern yourself with Wylder's welfare."

Earl stared at her in horror, wishing she'd keep her voice down. She brayed so loud, heads in their vicinity were beginning to turn toward it.

He didn't know what to say. He didn't like to be rude, even to Eulalia Culpepper. No lady deserved that, and he supposed if he stretched his imagination, he could consider her a lady.

But he felt trapped and, from the hard gleam in those eyes of hers, that's exactly what she'd set out to do—trap him.

"It does sound like a right good cause. But, Miss Eulalia, I was just preparing to ride up to the cabin for a spell."

"Come back in time for the benefit. You'll have four days. You know"—she fixed him with an even harder stare—"you don't go to church enough. I understand while you were sheriff you didn't have the time. Too many demands on you then. But now, you really should be seen as properly pious—"

"Pious? Me?"

"You have a reputation to maintain. Even though you've put all that dangerous work behind you, you're still a respected figure here in Wylder. It's decided, then. You'll come to the church supper with me. It's potluck, but don't you worry about that. I'm just off to order a pie from my girl, Cissy Standish."

Her girl? Word had it that before Cissy married the ex-gun-for-hire Buck Standish, Mrs. Culpepper had made the girl's life a misery. And he'd had that from Standish himself.

He, Earl, had to wiggle out of this. But how? He stared Eulalia Culpepper in the eye—kind of like facing down a wildcat—and said, "Ma'am, I regret to say I can't possibly accompany you."

"Can't?" she bleated. "Whyever not?"

Before he could come up with a plausible reason, the Morgans' door creaked open. Miss Vicky stood there, and a better sight Earl had rarely seen.

She wore a simple housedress he'd never glimpsed before, one with yellow flowers, and had all that red hair piled atop her head.

Funny, how two redheaded women could be so different. Miss Vicky sort of restored his faith in the breed.

She stepped out onto the rough, plank porch and gave him a look. "Earl?"

Just a single word, but it caused Mrs. Culpepper umbrage. An unmarried woman didn't call a man by his first name, or the other way round. Not without arguing a measure of familiarity.

He nodded at her. "Victoria. I was just comin' calling—"

Mrs. Culpepper gasped and took an outraged step backward—the right direction, so far as Earl was concerned. "What is this?"

Earl said, "I reckon you haven't met Miss Victoria Major—"

"Miss?"

"Newly arrived in town."

Victoria stepped out farther, coatless as she was, and seized Earl by the arm. She tipped up her chin and glared Eulalia Culpepper in the eye.

"I couldn't help but overhear your kind invitation to Earl. He won't be able to accept, on account of the fact that we—he and I—have an understanding. Tell her, Earl, darling."

That *darling* made Earl's knees go weak. For a minute, he felt sure he was going to dissolve in a puddle right there at the foot of the porch.

Eulalia huffed in distress. "You're courting this woman?"

"Uh—" Earl rarely stuttered. He did now, when he said, "I sh-sh-surely am."

Eulalia Culpepper swept Victoria with a look, up and down again. She sniffed. "You can do better, Earl Hanson."

"That's a damned—forgive me swearin'—rude thing to say." Earl wrapped an arm around Victoria and tugged her against him. "And I happen to think you're plum wrong."

Eulalia fixed him with a fierce stare. "I'll be keeping an eye on you, Earl Hanson. When I think you're ready for a real woman, I'll come calling."

She stomped off. Folks along the street pretended they hadn't been watching. Earl stood there with Victoria pressed to his side, figuring he should let go of her but not sure he wanted to.

Chapter Eleven

"Why'd you say that?" Earl asked Victoria. "That we have an understanding, I mean." He still hadn't let go of her, and Victoria's cheeks flamed. Not with embarrassment so much, even though people were staring. With—some other unidentified heat.

She stole a look into Earl's face. It was still half frozen and kind of hard to read.

"I could hear her screeching at you from inside the house. When I peeked out, it looked like you needed—well, rescue. Since you more or less rescued me at the saloon, I thought I should return the favor." Victoria hesitated. "Was I wrong?"

"No, ma'am, I reckon not. Seems I did need rescuin' from that woman."

"Who is she?"

"Eulalia Culpepper, widow and proprietress of the boarding house down on the corner. Coyote must be right."

"Coyote?"

"The doc, Doc Sullivan. He said she'd set her cap at me."

"Oh. I should say that's a correct assumption. If ever I saw a woman set her cap at a man, it's that one."

Earl let go of her, and spread his arms. "Can you tell me why? I'm old and grizzled. My knees are shot, and I don't have much else to recommend me."

Victoria eyed him slowly from those bright blue eyes downward. "Don't look so bad, to me."

"Miss Vicky—"

"Apparently Mrs. Culpepper's decided you'd do her just fine."

"Now that I'm out of the dangerous job of sheriffing."

Victoria gazed away in the direction Mrs. Culpepper had gone. In for a penny, in for a dollar. "She seems a very determined woman. Given that, I think we should maintain our ruse for the time being."

"Our ruse?"

"That we're—well, courting."

"Ah." Earl gave Victoria a long and very thoughtful look. For one breathless moment, she thought he'd refuse. But he said, "In that case, it might be seemly if we were seen out together."

"Oh?" She met his gaze.

"Yup. For instance, you might go to lunch with me."

"Lunch?"

"At Jake's. That's the diner over on Sidewinder Lane."

"I know. But—" She eyed Ulysses, standing by patiently. "You look like you're leaving. I thought you stopped here to say goodbye."

"Changed my mind. Miss Victoria, you run back inside and get your coat. I'll take Ulysses on back to the livery and call round for you in a few minutes."

Victoria's heart bounded. "We're going now?"

"Ain't no time like the present."

****

"This is very kind of you, Mr. Hanson."

"Better keep calling me Earl." Earl leaned his head closer to Victoria's across the table, and spoke in a whisper. "Make it seem intimate-like."

Her gaze flew to his. What eyes the woman had! Wide and so pale as to be considered colorless, with black rings around the iris. "Intimate?"

"Convincing." His gaze hovered at her lips.

"Oh, I think that would be a very good idea." She laid her hand on the table, and he covered it with his. "Anything to stave off the terrible Mrs. Culpepper. How long's she been a widow?"

"Long as I've been here in Wylder. She's been running that boarding house of hers ever since I moved here, eight years ago." Earl didn't remove his fingers from hers.

"So you don't know what happened to Mr. Culpepper?"

"I do not, though it fair stuns the mind."

"Think of the possibilities! She may have bludgeoned him. Or fed him something that got rid of him."

"Or he may just have taken death as the easy way out."

Victoria giggled. Earl couldn't mistake it for anything but a giggle.

He grinned. "Lord forgive me saying such things."

Victoria's gaze clung to his. "I think it would prove most convincing—of our supposed relationship, I mean—if you would return to the saloon and play with me tonight."

The shocking thought occurred to Earl that he'd like to play with her. All night. Oh, what in tarnation was the matter with him?

"It'll be busy tonight, no doubt."

"All the better. More eyes to see us."

"Hmm." It made a good excuse to spend the evening with her. But was that wise, with such wild thoughts running round in his head?

He was a man who'd long ago learned to discipline his impulses. At least he believed he had, before Miss Victoria Major came along. Now he found he had the impulse to lean right across the table and press his lips against her pale cheek, to thread his fingers through hers. To maybe take her up and show her the lonely cabin beneath the pines, see what she thought of it.

Whoa, old man, he told himself much as he might speak to Ulysses. Don't get ahead of yourself.

"I reckon I might sit in for a few songs, help keep the rowdies at bay. But it's your show, Miss Vicky."

She smiled, a real smile that seemed to light her from within. "If it's my show, that means I can invite who I like. And—I do believe I want you there."

Good enough, Earl thought. Good enough.

****

Earl had been right, and the crowd that night proved a wild one. The small, friendly group who'd ridden out the storm together last evening appeared to have melted away, replaced by a variety of rowdies, hard drinkers, and cowhands spoiling for trouble.

As a result, Earl slipped into what Victoria could only call his sheriff persona. Like a watchdog, he occupied the chair beside her and kept a fierce eye on everything. She played, trying her best to overlook the violence and please the customers with her ever-expanding repertoire.

Except, that was, when the violence came too

close. Near the end of the evening, when she swore nearly everybody in the place was roaring drunk, a fist fight broke out between two of the patrons. She missed what started it—a card game, most likely, since she'd learned those caused most dust-ups. But it came spilling across the room with enormous velocity, the combatants hurtling directly toward the piano.

Suddenly, Earl was on his feet. With deceptive speed, he imposed his body between Victoria and the wranglers. When they crashed into him, his hands came up and collared the nearest, and gave him a shake.

"Watch where you're going, you rapscallions! There's a lady present."

Victoria, who'd stopped playing abruptly, shrank back. Never before had she been so close to flowing blood and raw, masculine anger. She watched as Earl shoved the men away, his hand immediately flying to hover over his gun.

Why, he moved like a gunslinger, almost. Or a sheriff, she supposed.

The cowhands ultimately took it outside. Mr. Callahan, who appeared almost magically, crossed over to speak with Earl.

"Thanks for that, Sheriff. They'd have wrecked the place."

"I ain't the sheriff," Earl retorted, sounding crabby.

"Well, I'm grateful all the same." Billy Callahan gave Victoria a visual inspection. "Miss Major, you all right?"

"A bit shaken, that's all."

"Those rogues didn't hurt you none?"

"No, thanks to Mr. Hanson."

Mr. Callahan said, "Tomorrow's Sunday. Why

don't you take the evening off?"

"Truly?"

"You haven't had a night off since you arrived, have you?"

Earl spoke up. "How will you keep those animals corralled and calm without music?"

"I don't know, but it occurs to me Miss Major could use a respite."

"Thank you very much." Suddenly Victoria wanted nothing more than to be away from this place. Well, maybe she wanted one thing more. If she stayed away from the Trail's End, she wouldn't see Earl.

Earl, who made her feel so safe. And who prompted a hundred other emotions.

"Come on, pack up your music. Evening's over," he told her.

Walking home, she had no excuse to take hold of his arm. The snow had cleared. In truth, he had no excuse to walk her home either, yet he did. And when she took his arm anyway, he tucked her in closer to his side.

At Hattie's door, she turned to face him. "Thank you, Earl, for protecting me. That could have been quite nasty." She couldn't expect him to keep playing guard at her side, though.

He just nodded, not looking at her. Instead he seemed to eye the stars overhead. "Looks like it may be fine weather tomorrow. What you planning to do with your day off?"

"Oh, I don't know." She should wash some unmentionables. And she had letters to write.

His gaze focused on her face. His moustache twitched. "How'd you like to take a ride out? If the weather holds, that is."

"A ride? With you?"

"With me, yes."

"I'd like that very much."

"Good. You haven't seen much of the country hereabouts. And I thought you might like to see my cabin."

"Your—cabin." Victoria's pulse fluttered.

"Seems like the kind of thing a courting couple might do, don't it?"

"Oh. Well, yes." Victoria fought her immediate disappointment. Was he just playacting? Of course he was.

"If you're amenable, Miss Vicky, I'll rent a wagon from the livery and come pick you up. Say around noon?"

"That—that would be just fine. And yes, I'm amenable."

"That's set, then. Have a pleasant night, Miss Victoria."

"Good night, Earl."

Greatly daring, Victoria leaned up and kissed him on the cheek. Just a quick peck, she meant it as a show of gratitude.

Nothing, nothing more.

Chapter Twelve

Earl squinted at the sky as he directed the team and wagon through the Sunday morning streets of Wylder. He'd jumped the gun a bit in his eagerness to see Miss Vicky. It wasn't quite noon. But the weather that had looked so clear and promising last night had begun clouding up after daybreak in an ominous fashion, out over the hills in the direction they'd be traveling.

He didn't want to miss his day out with Victoria. He surely did not. He told himself it was for her sake— she'd had precious little of what he could call enjoyment since coming to Wylder. And she deserved it. Not that he supposed a ride out to see that cabin of his could compete with the experiences of her past. Concerts and plays and such. But hell, it was all he had to offer.

He drew the team up in front of the Morgans' place, wondering if she'd be ready yet. Whether she'd changed her mind. Maybe, upon reflection, she'd decided his proposal was improper.

Damn, but he'd be mighty disappointed if she had. Because he could still feel the kiss she'd planted on him last night. It had been a sweet, chaste thing, sure— nothing more than a mark of gratitude. But it had burned in a way that assured he kept thinking on it all night.

How long since he'd felt like this? And oh, Lord, if

a peck on the cheek did this to him, what about a proper kiss on the lips?

He wouldn't find out, mainly because a proper kiss wouldn't be—well, proper. But he wanted to.

Might be a good reason to cancel the day's plans—if the skies out over the hills didn't make a better one.

Before he could reason it out further, the door of the house creaked open, and Victoria peered out. A smile came to her face, one that made her look like a girl.

He leaped down from the wagon seat, moving like a young man. "Miss Vicky."

"Earl."

People on the street, most on their way home from church and some headed for the saloon—the two Wylder factions, so to speak—stared. Well, that was the whole point of this, wasn't it?

Wasn't it?

She stepped out. Earl noted she wore her heavy coat and carried a sort of muff in one hand. But she planted her other hand firmly in his as he helped her up into the wagon and climbed up after her.

He meant to say something about the weather, to warn her that the beautiful morning might be fleeting. But she turned to him with those pale eyes of hers alight, and said, "I'm so excited to see the countryside. I do believe this will do me a powerful amount of good."

Earl just jiggled the reins and urged the team back on up the street.

"It's very kind of you," Victoria said.

Kind. She tended to call him that quite a lot. He might have to set her straight in that regard, because he wouldn't want her getting the wrong idea about him.

"How long did you say you've lived in Wylder?" she asked as they rode.

"About eight years or so. But I'm no stranger to towns like this, see. My father was a doctor. We lived in several frontier settlements over the years, till I got fed up with being told what to do and lit out on my own. He ended up his career doctoring right here, in Wylder."

"Oh." She looked interested. "You didn't want to follow in your father's footsteps and study medicine, too?"

"That's right—you followed your own father into a musical career, didn't you?"

"Yes, though I was never a touch on the musician he was."

"I had a wild streak when I was young. Thought it a fine thing to make my way with my guns. After that—well, once I got sick of killing men, I lived for a time in a cabin not unlike the one we'll be seeing today. It was all a long while ago." He drew a breath. "I'm fifty-six." Might as well get that out of the way, let her know she was dealing with an old man. One mostly used up, with bad knees and a body that wasn't quite as strong or agile as it used to be.

She shifted a bit on the seat beside him. "I'm almost forty-eight. I know a lady isn't supposed to tell her age, but—well, I'd prefer us to be honest with each other."

"Me too."

"And how'd you wind up back in the same town where your father was doctor?" She gave him a sympathetic look. "I assume he's gone, now?"

"Dead." Earl nodded. "Doc Sullivan's took over from him." He slanted a look at her. "You were right fond of your father, were you?"

"Oh, yes. I admired him immensely, and I followed him, as you say, even when I should perhaps have made a life of my own."

"My relationship with my pa was...complicated. He was a man of strong opinions, and never hesitated to voice 'em. Trouble was, his opinions were always right, and no amount of talking could persuade him differently. A young man"—he squinted his eyes, looking back at the past—"reaches a point where he don't want to take that anymore. It's funny, Miss Vicky—I never thought I'd want to come to Wylder, just 'cause he was here. But yeah, he's gone now. And against all odds, I settled in."

Now that he came to study on it, it seemed he'd lived an unsettled life, despite his many gigs as sheriff in various towns. Always following the urging of that inner wild streak, maybe. But a man of fifty-six had no right to own a wild streak.

She asked softly, "You never married, then?"

He shot her a look. Would she be shocked by the truth? But she'd asked for honesty.

He jiggled the reins across the horses' backs. "I did, though not legal-like."

"What's that mean? Oh—you lived with a woman outside the bonds of—"

"Wedlock. Though we were as good as married. Seemed that way to me and to her, I think. Like I say, it was a long time ago."

They rode in silence for several minutes. "What happened to her?"

"Died." Earl didn't want to think about that. It hurt too much even now.

"You never married again?"

"Nope."

"Most people do, so I've found. It's like they have a terror of being alone. Most the time, the second unions don't really work out all that well."

"There are often children to be raised. And chores to be shared."

"A terrible reason to marry."

"That why you kept away from it, Miss Vicky?"

She gave a hard laugh. "I'm afraid not. The truth is, only one person ever asked me, and I turned him down."

"I find that hard to believe, that you didn't have a heap of offers, I mean."

"You shouldn't. I can't dance, and stuck behind the keyboard most my life, I've had few opportunities. I don't simper, or play the games women must to attract a husband. I'm plain and ordinary, and I guess my heart's always had an independent streak also."

"You didn't want to settle."

"I most assuredly did not. Besides, I never minded my own company much."

"Me, either."

"Better alone than with the wrong person, just for the sake of it."

"A sound philosophy."

"I hope you don't mind me asking—how did your wife die?"

"I don't mind. She died trying to give me a son. They both died." It had been winter then, also. Just the two—three—of them alone in the ramshackle cabin. No help within fifty miles. He'd done what he could and failed miserably.

What had seemed like a good idea at the time—living in isolation—had cost Little Bird her life.

What if he made a similarly rash choice now?

"I'm sorry to hear that. So," she asked, with some emphasis, "you never—well, fell in love again?"

"Love, me? Who would want a grizzled old specimen like me?"

"Mrs. Culpepper, obviously."

They grinned at one another.

"I guess," she said carefully, "we're just two plain misfits."

"I reckon you're right." And he suspected that's why they fit so well together.

Chapter Thirteen

By the time they reached the cabin, it had started to snow, beautiful little flakes that swirled down to contrast starkly with the deep green of the pines that clustered around the place. The air felt colder, too—so cold it stung.

Victoria wasn't sure what she'd expected. It wasn't this. Earl said he'd built the cabin for his retirement, yet it looked as if it had grown there, part of the setting.

The last leg of the journey had been a climb that taxed the horses. The cabin sat half way up a hillside and peeked out from its perch onto a stunning outlook below.

"Oh, my goodness," Victoria said as soon as Earl helped her down from the wagon. "This is magnificent!"

"You like it?"

"Who wouldn't? You can just stand here and see forever."

"Never thought of it that way, but I reckon you're right." He paused beside her, and they gazed back down the hill, shoulder to shoulder. He rumbled, "Right now, all I can see is snow."

"Well, maybe not all, but it has picked up, hasn't it?"

"Let me show you inside. Then I'll shelter the horses in Ulysses' lean-to. Don't expect too much, now," he warned as he opened the door. "I haven't had a chance to what you'd call settle the place."

The interior of the cabin consisted of one good-sized room and, yes, it was what Victoria would call stark. A big, river-stone fireplace dominated one wall, with a settle at one side and a big brass bed on the other. She could see no kitchen as such, but a range of wooden shelves occupied one wall. Big, bark-covered timbers soared overhead, and but a single window admitted light.

"It's charming."

"You think so?" Earl sounded pleased.

"I do."

"It needs—aww, I don't know—some things adding in. Possessions, maybe. A woman's touch."

A woman's touch. She was a woman.

"It needs to feel lived-in, that's all. It has great bones."

"Well, perhaps so. Let me get a fire going, so you can get warm." He set Louise, whom he'd brought along, over against the wall.

"I can do that. You go settle the horses. We can't leave the poor creatures standing in the cold."

"You sure?"

"Certain."

"That's right considerate of you."

He went out, and Victoria shivered. The interior of the cabin felt colder than outside. Leaving her coat on, she went and laid a fire in the enormous hearth, using supplies from the woodbox at one side.

Almost immediately, Earl stepped back in.

"Miss Victoria, I'm thinking we maybe should reconsider our venture. Snow's coming down harder.

Better we turn right around and head back for town."

Victoria's heart fell. "Already? But it was such a fine day."

"Storm's coming over the mountains. It does that sometimes, without much warning."

"Storm?"

His moustache twitched. "Looks that way. I apologize, Miss Vicky. I read the weather plum wrong."

"Not your fault. If we head back now, might the storm catch us?"

"Could do."

"Well, that seems rather precipitous, then. Wouldn't be good for us or the team. We've reached shelter here. Maybe we should stay put."

"Might be the smart thing to do. But, Miss Vicky, if we try and wait it out, I can't promise I'll get you back to Wylder tonight."

"Oh."

"I know we're playing at courting here, but that would put paid to your reputation."

Playing at courting. Well, had she seriously hoped for more?

"My reputation," she repeated bitterly. She needed to tell him the truth. But—well, she liked the way he looked at her. She didn't want that to change. "I suppose people will talk?"

"They surely will."

"Mr. Earl, I'm a forty-eight-year-old spinster who's pounding piano keys in a saloon for a living. Do you truly think I care?"

****

The weather blew. It wasn't what Earl would call a

blizzard, as such. One of those could last for days and render the roads impassable for even longer. No, this was just a kiss from a passing storm.

Yet he chastised himself. He should have known better, read the weather more accurately, in order to protect Miss Victoria's reputation.

He'd been too eager to spend the day with her, eager to show off this place he'd built, like a little kid.

Did he fancy Miss Victoria? Seemed ridiculous, on the face of it. Him, an old man. You'd think all such impulses would have flown.

But shut inside with her, beside the fire and with that wind moaning outside, well, he got thoughts.

In an effort to distract himself as much as Victoria, he suggested a game of cards. They sat at the rough wooden table while he tried to teach her the rules of poker. But he found himself watching her hands—pale and slender they were, just like the rest of her—and imagining them touching him. Which didn't do a damn thing for his self-control.

"Tell me about yourself, Miss Vicky." Perhaps if they talked, he could get his head straight.

Her hands froze. She'd enjoyed a run of beginner's luck, somewhat spoiled by her continually asking him *what* beat *what*. "There's not much to tell."

"Must be." She said she was almost forty-eight. That someone had asked her to marry him, and she'd turned him down. She would have had woes and triumphs. "You said your pa played piano too."

"Yes. John Major. He was famous all through the East. We traveled a lot. Went from concert hall to concert hall. I accompanied him."

"You his only child?"

"No. I have an older brother. He left home early—just as you did." Did her voice tighten, when she said this?

"And your ma?"

"She—she and my father went their separate ways when I was twelve."

"I see." Earl truly didn't. In his estimation, men and women stayed married, even when they shouldn't. For better or worse, in fact. Once hitched, likely only death split them.

"She lives with my brother now." Victoria's clear eyes lifted to Earl's. "We chose, you see. Ron to go with Mother, and I with Father."

"Ah." Earl contemplated it. "You ever regret that choice?"

"There have been times in my life when I've regretted everything. And"—she smiled tremulously—"times when I haven't."

"I hear that." Earl contemplated it.

The eldest of his parents' brood, he'd always seemed to have a lot of responsibility heaped on him. His ma had told him she'd be happy if he made something of himself. *Be a man*, as she'd put it. He supposed that had stuck with him, even maybe urged him to trade his outlaw guns for ones on the other side of the law.

Had he become anything? Sheriff, for a while. No longer. Dang!

"Sounds like an interesting life," he offered, "traveling around that way."

"It was. I loved hearing Father play. In fact I think that's why I chose him over Mother, for the sake of his music. But—he was a curious man. Very, very focused.

He didn't care for much except performing, when it came down to it."

"Must have cared for you."

"I sometimes wonder. Because, you know, he gave very little thought to me. To my comfort, my education or my—my future. To whether I wanted to move on to the next town. To what would happen to me after—after I stopped following him.

"But oh, Earl, you should have heard him play! We could have just finished an argument—we tended to argue a lot, though it never got me anywhere—and I'd be so angry. But when he started playing Chopin—"

"That's your favorite, is it? Chopin?"

She nodded.

"You play it too?"

"I'm adequate. Not the master he was."

"You'll have to play some for me, when we get back to town."

"I will. But it can't match the experience of sitting in a concert hall and listening while the music just flowed from him. It—it transported me."

Again she hesitated, and rearranged the cards in her hand. "Sometimes I think I should have fought harder."

"How so?"

"For a life of my own. The life I did have revolved around Father. No—no time for suitors. No plans. I became, in essence, his handmaiden. And when he was gone—my life, having revolved around him, was empty."

"If you don't mind me asking, what happened to him?"

"They said it was consumption. He went slowly. Turned into a ghost right before my eyes." She smiled bleakly. "He kept playing right till the end."

"Miss Vicky, I'm sorry to have reminded you of all this."

"No need to remind me. It's in my mind every day. When I wake up in the morning and—and when I go to bed at night."

Earl frowned. "What did you do, after? You said you sometimes played along with him, when he was still alive."

"Yes. It was like a parlor trick—the great John Major and his daughter. Twin pianos on the stage. But that's all it was. I quickly discovered, after he passed, I could get no jobs on my own name. I found myself in St. Louis, Missouri. I had no way to feed myself and no place to live."

"He must have had a bit put aside, surely?" Even Earl had managed to salt some money away, on his measly sheriff's salary.

"Very little. Father liked to live big, to the limit of his income. A new suit for every performance, the best of rooms at every hotel, and lavish dinners."

And he, Earl, had hoped to impress this woman at Jake's. She was out of his reach, surely—as if he'd imagined otherwise.

"I was able to sell most of his clothing. Liquidate his cuff links and other tidbits. After that, I had to take jobs clerking. That was hand-to-mouth, and I was miserable at it."

"When did you start teaching?"

"That happened by accident. I overheard a woman in the shop telling another she wanted her daughter to take piano lessons. I volunteered my services and took on a few students, for extra money. Not much money, though. You'd be surprised how miserly wealthy women can be."

"I'll bet."

"When I heard about an opening at one of my students' schools, I applied and was hired. It came with a room, which solved one big problem. But such positions are terribly insecure. I kept getting struck off. Several of the academies closed down."

"Sounds like a perilous existence."

"It was, truly. And no chance to—well, to settle."

"You say you regret your choices."

"Some of them."

"You regret coming to Wylder, now?"

She settled those clear, pale eyes on him and took a moment to contemplate the question before she answered. "No, Earl. I don't believe I do."

Chapter Fourteen

Hard pellets of snow tapped against the cabin's single window, and Victoria moved restlessly between the blankets. Earl had insisted she take the bed—his bed—for the night, while he bunked on the settle. She'd attempted to argue him out of it, saying she'd fit much better on the narrow settle, but to no avail.

"Won't hear of it," he'd told her sweepingly. "We'll keep things this way, all right and proper."

Only it wasn't right and proper, was it? At least, in the eyes of anyone who couldn't actually see them now. When she went back to Wylder tomorrow—as presumably she would—folks would know only that they'd been away together overnight.

Scandal. Again.

Heat flooded over her at the thought of it, there in the quiet cabin. She should have told Earl about that other scandal which trailed behind her like a cloud of dirty smoke. It had been the perfect opportunity. They'd been talking about her past. She could have slipped it in, all casual. Only she didn't feel casual about it. And sharing it with Earl—well, it could change everything, including the way he looked at her.

Oh, but she liked the way he looked at her! She did believe no other man had ever regarded her in such a fashion.

She stirred again, and the quiet deepened. She

could hear the fire popping as the embers settled from orange to gray. She could hear Earl breathing, low and steady.

What would he do if she woke him now and told him she had something else to share? What if this storm had been sent just to give her that opportunity? Because Earl Hanson seemed an honest man. And before she developed deeper feelings for him, she owed him the truth.

Either that or she must walk away. Thank him for his help at the Trail's End, tell him they shouldn't see each other anymore.

Only she didn't believe that. On the contrary, she could glimpse something beautiful and dazzling hovering over the horizon of their relationship like a shimmering sunrise. Friendship, maybe. More than friendship—well, not if she chose to send him away.

She thrashed once more and turned over. Earl's voice came out of the darkness.

"You all right there, Miss Victoria?"

"Um—yes. Why do you ask?"

"Just that you seem terrible restless. If you need the outhouse—"

"It isn't that." Victoria sat up in the bed. Earl lifted up onto his elbow on the settle, maybe ten feet between them.

"Can't sleep?"

"I seem to be having trouble."

"Happens that way sometimes, in a strange place."

"I didn't mean to disturb you."

"That's all right. Over the years, I've got used to gettin' my sleep interrupted. Seems like I'd just fall into a deep snooze and my deputy would come runnin', saying some damn fool was drunk and breaking heads in the Five Star, or shootin' up the street."

"I see."

"You feel like talking?"

"I do, actually." Best to get this burden off her chest now, while she had the chance. Even if it did wreck things between them.

She got up out of the bed, trailing one of the blankets behind her. Nothing improper about it—she was still fully dressed except for her shoes. So was Earl, though he'd removed his vest and his shirt was open at the throat. Without his hat, his silver hair spilled across his forehead, and the firelight played hide-and-seek with his expression.

She parked in a chair at the table, and felt him staring.

"Mercy, Miss Vicky."

"Eh?"

"That hair of yorn!"

Oh, right. She had taken it down before she retired, not wanting the hairpins to stab her in the head during the night. It flowed over her shoulders and down her back.

"It's an awful color, isn't it? I always got picked on in school."

"It's a right glorious color, especially in this firelight."

"Oh. Well, thank you." She'd like to sit here and soak up his admiration. Imagine he looked at her with approval. Instead, she had to disabuse any ideas he had about her character.

"Earl, I'm grateful for your friendship. I'm not mistaken, am I, in thinking that's what you've offered me? Your protection at the saloon and—and your company while playing music."

His voice turned cautious. "That's right."

"And—and friends, they're honest with each other."

"Well, right. Usually."

"I should have told you this early on, when we were speaking together so earnestly. I'm not the woman you think."

He took a moment to ponder that before he said, "And, Miss Vicky, how do you know just what sort of woman I think you be?"

"I'm assuming you think I'm proper. Respectable." Madness to sit in a mountain cabin with a man, shut in by the storm, and tell him she wasn't respectable. "I mean," she hurried on, "you've always treated me with a great deal of respect—"

"You tellin' me you don't deserve that?"

"Maybe not. You spoke about scandal erupting in town, when we return. Well, I already have a measure of dark scandal following me."

"Is that so?"

"Yes. It's the reason I left my last post, and a large part of the reason I came west."

"Trouble, you mean? Why didn't you tell me?"

"As I say, I was afraid—afraid it would change how you perceive me."

"Well, Miss Vicky, I perceive you in a number of different ways. To be frank, I think you're a complicated woman, with some conflicts all balled up inside you. So whatever you have to say may not surprise me as much as you suppose."

What a generous thing for him to say, when he

hadn't even heard her out. She flushed with warmth and trembled inwardly.

"At the last place I worked, Miss Angelina's School for Young Women in Kansas City, I taught piano. And there was a young dancing master, there just on trial, you see. Mistress Millicent Goldstone, who ran the school, seldom hired young men, it being a distraction for the students. But she needed someone, and he turned up with good credentials.

"And oh, was he handsome!" Victoria thought on Matthew's tall frame, his dark hair and eyes that could flash with the devil's own mirth. Had she been taken in by him?

Earl twitched, but said nothing.

"Millicent said there was something about him, something that bothered her. She held off from hiring him outright. He wanted that place, though, and badly. I now wonder why."

"Maybe runnin' from something?"

"Probably. Another scandal, most likely. Anyway, Matthew was very, very nice to me. I know now that was because he saw how close Millicent and I were, and wanted me to put in a good word for him. But I was—" Victoria became stuck.

"Flattered?"

"Flattered, yes, even though it was utterly ridiculous, thinking he could actually be interested in me. I was old enough to be his mother."

"But you weren't. His mother, I mean. So— feelings sprang up?"

"Yes. He bowled me over with his attention. His compliments. Little smiles just for me. I know, it's laughable."

"It isn't."

She pressed her hands to her face. "I'm embarrassed just admitting it. Admitting it to you."

"Why to me?"

"Because." Honesty was wanted here. "I admire you. And I hate for you to see me as a silly old woman who was taken in."

"You ain't that. Not silly. Or old."

Victoria laughed unsteadily. "You're a kind man, Earl Hanson."

"I've seen a lot. And heard a lot. What happened?"

"I can't say."

"He seduce you?"

Victoria's gaze flew to Earl's. His blue eyes had narrowed. Did he seek to judge her? Surely not.

"No. At least—not completely. I've never—never been with a man, if you know what I mean." Her cheeks flamed.

"I do."

"But—but there were secret meetings. Stolen kisses. Looking back on it, I can't believe I ever thought—well, that he was sincerely interested in me. Maybe I knew, all the while, that he wasn't. I merely got—"

"Swept away?"

"Yes. How many nights I've wept over it, since!"

"Crying never does much good, in my experience."

"No, it does not. Anyway, we got caught by a number of students. It blew up then, just like a keg of nitroglycerin. It spread from student to student, and the students informed their parents. Millicent had no choice but to dismiss me. She had parents hollering, saying I set a bad example for their girls. It was true."

"I see. And him—this Matthew fella?"

"He blamed me. He stood there bold as brass and said that I seduced him. That I'd led him astray. Me! Everyone believed him. He went on to take another post in the city. But I—I was ostracized. I couldn't get a place washing dishes after that."

"Don't seem fair."

"It wasn't. But the harder I tried to defend myself, the worse it got. People said things like, 'The lady doth protest too much.' And the girls who had seen us—their descriptions became lurid. I tried applying for work in other cities, but every respectable place wants references. Eventually, I ran out of money. Millicent couldn't let me stay with her, but she did give me train fare west."

"And you already knew the Morgans, here in Wylder?"

"Yes. I thought relocating so far west would suit me well. But even in Wylder, jobs haven't been easy to come by. After failing at waitressing and a couple other positions, I saw the sign saying they needed a piano player at the Trail's End."

"I see." Earl got up and stirred the fire, sending up a shower of orange sparks before he added a log.

When he sat back down, Victoria told him, "Go ahead. Say it."

"Say what?"

"That in light of this, we can no longer be friends."

He tipped his head. "Was I gonna say that?"

"I don't know. Maybe you should. My reputation's ruined. And it's bound to follow me wherever I go."

"A reputation's a funny thing. I used to have one. Now, I've got another—as sheriff. Folks are having trouble letting go of that one, but I reckon I feel another one comin' on. Post-sheriff, if you want to call it that.

"And I'll tell you, Miss Vicky, for all those things folks think of me, few of them really know me. The Earl Hanson that dwells inside, that is. Folks see what they want to see. And if that's the case, I reckon a reputation don't matter so much, does it? It's just a coat you wear."

"An awfully important coat."

"No question. But one that you can maybe swap for another."

"This has cost me my career."

"Has it? You're still playin' piano. And I reckon when a little time passes, you could start giving private lessons again, to them as can afford it. Wylder's not like other places. It's kind of forgiving. And it turns a blind eye to what's come before."

Victoria blew out a breath. He'd heard her story— the worst of her—and he hadn't turned away. Not yet.

"Well, but now if we return to town, having spent the…the night together…" She stumbled there.

Earl rubbed his chin. "There is that."

"People are bound to start asking questions. And if the rest of it comes out—"

"Won't," Earl said comfortably. He leaned forward and widened his eyes at Victoria. "And if folks start calling your reputation into question, I guess I'll just have to do something about it."

Chapter Fifteen

"You ready to leave?" Earl shot a look at Victoria,
who stood beside him. Clear mountain light spilled over
her, turning that pale complexion of hers to ivory and
her hair—

Oh, Lord, that hair! When he'd seen it in the
firelight last night, spilling loose like that all down her
back and shoulders, well, it had started a buzz the like
of which he'd not felt in years. She might think that
Matthew fellow had played her. Earl suspected he
might just have given in to some plain, old-fashioned
temptation.

Earl nearly had, last night. He'd wanted nothing
more than to lean forward from his seat on the settle
and kiss her. To run his fingers through her hair. But a
man didn't push himself on a woman, especially one
unloading worries about her reputation.

Unforgivable. That didn't keep him from wanting
to kiss her even now.

He was a man used to taking care of things, solving
problems. And he felt pretty sure he could take care of
Miss Vicky. But only if she wanted that.

She talked about making some bad choices in the
past, but she had in fact made those choices—as an
independent woman did. He had no right to step in and
take any part of that away from her.

There were biddable women, like Little Bird had

been, and unbiddable ones like Eulalia Culpepper. He figured Miss Vicky fell somewhere between.

He didn't want to put a foot wrong.

"I almost hate to leave." Victoria turned as he helped her up into the wagon, and looked at the cabin. "I like it here."

"Do you?" He liked having her here, way too much. He had thoughts of the two of them sharing the big brass bed, and all her red hair wrapped around them.

"It's comfortable. I'm surprised you can tear yourself away."

"Well, I'll tell you, Miss Vicky, it gets lonely." He dared add, "Though it didn't feel lonely with you here."

Could she tell what he was thinking? Ah, it was madness. He couldn't expect a woman like Victoria Major—cultured and educated—to be happy in a mountain cabin with an old, grizzled specimen like him.

"Do you think people will talk, Earl, when we ride back into town?"

Did he think people would talk? Did birds fly? Did rams get horny in the spring?

"Well, now. I just hope your friend, Mrs. Morgan, ain't overly concerned. You told her you'd be back yesterday, didn't you?"

"I'm not sure I said. But she would have assumed, yes."

"Let's hope there's no furor."

There was furor. As they soon discovered, Hattie had gone to the sheriff when Victoria failed to return, and he'd instituted a search all over town, even though the storm made that difficult, and it was Branch Wylder's opinion Earl had held up somewhere to ride it out.

As a consequence, just about everybody in town knew Earl Hanson had absconded with the piano player from the Trail's End—the one he'd been seen sitting alongside while playing all those duets. Who would have thought it of Earl? That old dog! Truly, you'd think he'd be a little more discreet.

Earl listened to the talk with dismay. And there was more than just talk. Men stopped him on the street with knowing grins, and slapped him on the back. Women glared at him with glances sharp as knives.

It made him shudder, so it did, on Victoria's behalf.

He'd dropped her off at the Morgans' before taking the wagon and team back to the livery, where the proprietor, young Jackson Daniels, greeted him.

"Hey, Earl, everybody's lookin' for you. You and that piano-playin' woman. You didn't say you'd have the team out all night." Jackson peered into the back of the wagon. "Make a comfortable bed, did it?"

Earl resisted the urge to slug Daniels and moved on. But it was the same at Jake's, where he stopped for lunch. And at the mercantile, where he went for tobacco.

He debated long and hard over whether to turn up at the Trail's End that night. Victoria was due to play, and he wanted to make sure she didn't have a hard time. Would it look better or worse for him to be there?

Imagine worrying about ruining a woman's reputation at his time of life! Worst thing was, he wanted to ruin Miss Vicky's reputation. He wanted to ruin it real good.

Fool, he chastised himself. *Last thing that woman*

needs is a used-up ex-sheriff. Only, when he was around her he didn't feel used up. In fact, quite the contrary.

Might make a good reason for staying away from the saloon altogether.

But then he wouldn't know what was happening to her. Wouldn't have a chance to protect her if she needed it.

After considerable thought, he took himself back to the Morgans' house and knocked on the door.

When Hattie Morgan opened it and saw him, she looked indignant. "Sheriff Hanson, I am surprised you would show your face here. And I have to say, I am shocked by your most recent behavior. A man of your stature—"

"I'm not the sheriff no more."

"And you think that gives you license to ruin a woman's reputation? To drag her off to that cabin of yours and keep her there all night?"

"Now, Mrs. Morgan, you know there was a storm."

"And you should know better than to take Victoria off alone with you in such weather."

"You're right, and I'm plum sorry about that. But you know, Mrs. Morgan, this ain't a stuffy sort of town. If there's talk, it will die down quick enough."

"Some of us are trying to be respectable!"

"I know that." It was one of the defining characteristics of Wylder, a town trying to overcome its rough-and-tumble roots and become respectable. Just as he had. Or had he? It seemed that streak of wild that had taken him from his boyhood home still lingered, deep inside.

What he'd thought he had well-disciplined maybe

wasn't.

"I'd like to see her, Mrs. Morgan, make sure she's all right."

"She isn't." Mrs. Morgan tried to shut the door in Earl's face.

He planted his palm against the boards. "Please. Just for a minute."

She sniffed. "Come into the parlor. People are staring."

So they were. Earl took a peek over his shoulder as he went in. Avid stares, plenty of them.

The parlor felt cold and little used. Earl paced back and forth, his knees aching, while he listened to a muffled conversation from the next room. Couldn't catch the words, just the tone.

At last, Victoria stepped in. He could see right away she'd been crying, and it felt like a stab to his heart.

He turned and faced her, his hat in his hands. "Miss Victoria, I'm right regretful about all this. I'm a fool."

Her gaze darted to his and as quickly away again. Not a good sign. "Tom is very angry. Says I've brought dishonor on his house. He wanted to toss me out, but Hattie persuaded him not to."

"Is that so?"

She nodded miserably. "Says I'm a bad influence on the children. Seems I'm destined to be a bad influence, one way or another."

"Looks like I'll have to have a talk with old Tom." The number of times he, Earl, in his capacity of sheriff had seen Tom Morgan sneaking into the Wylder County Social Club might just reach Hattie's ears if Tom insisted on remaining indignant.

"Oh, please don't. There's already been one terrible bust-up. I couldn't bear another one."

"All right." But he'd keep it in his back pocket, so to speak.

She wrung her hands. "I confess, I don't know what to do. I could face it out." She tipped up her chin. "But I'm feeling rather battered and don't know if I have the courage."

"You have plenty of courage, Vicky."

"Or I could pack up my things, get out of Tom's house the way he wants, and go."

Earl's heart clenched. "Go? Go where?"

She shrugged. "What's the next stop down the line?"

"Laramie."

"Maybe there."

Laramie wouldn't be so bad. With Ulysses' help, he could still see her.

"Or farther west."

"Now you listen here. This is all my fault. Let me see if I can speak some words in a few ears—"

"Fight my battle for me?"

"Not for you, Vicky. *With* you."

She smiled, but it looked bleak. "I don't think that would go very far in stopping the gossip, do you? We probably shouldn't be seen together again."

"Oh." God damn it!

"Just until I make up my mind whether I'm leaving Wylder or not."

"I was going to ask if you wanted me at the saloon tonight. I guess the answer is no."

"I would like having you there, most assuredly. But think how the tongues would wag."

Earl didn't care about the tongues, but it was plain she did. For a woman fleeing scandal, this had to be her worst nightmare.

But…damn it!

"All right," he said slowly. "But I don't think you should run." Again. He didn't add that, but she heard it anyway.

"Didn't work too well last time, did it?"

"No, Miss Vicky." Earl swallowed hard. "I reckon you've got two choices. You can stay and face down the talk—or you can stay and marry me."

Chapter Sixteen

Victoria blinked at the man standing there before her in the Morgans' parlor. Yes, he was Earl Hanson, all right, with his silvery hair, grizzled sideburns, and that fantastically luxurious moustache. And what had Earl Hanson just said?

He'd asked her to marry him.

A pang very like that she imagined preceded a heart attack pierced her chest. Her first proposal of marriage since Roger Trent, who had never loved her. From a man she very much admired, one whose company she valued enormously.

Given out of pity. Because Earl Hanson did not love her, either.

Gazing into his impossibly blue eyes, she tried to see something besides pity there. He liked her, certainly. And she suspected he felt protective. A man like him would. He also felt responsible for her current predicament.

Was that all? He guarded his expression too well for her to tell.

But it had to be…pity. A sense of responsibility. Not love. No one had ever fallen in love with Victoria Major.

No one ever would. She puffed out a breath of regret. Her next thought, though, stunned her: *She could take him up on it.*

Oh, heavens. Oh, heavens! She could become Earl Hanson's wife.

That prospect knocked the wind right out of her, so she gaped at him like a fish on a hook.

"Well?" He shuffled his feet. "Say something, Miss Victoria."

"I—uh—"

She couldn't possibly say yes. She discovered, much to her surprise, she didn't want to say no. He might be weathered and, yes, grizzled, but this was a true man standing in front of her. Could she say no to such a man?

Yet she suspected his motives. She truly did.

She could see something else in his eyes now, right enough. He looked worried. That she'd turn him down? Or that she wouldn't?

"Earl, I understand you feel responsible for my situation and all the talk here in town. That's no reason for you to—to offer me marriage."

Say that's not why, not why you offered, she begged him silently. *Tell me there's more.*

"Ain't it? But in a lot of places—maybe not Wylder—it's expected, when a man damages a woman's reputation."

She closed her eyes on a wave of pain.

"And, Victoria, it would solve your other problem as well, concerning the school scandal. I ain't much, but I reckon at this point in my life I'd make a sufficiently respectable husband."

Victoria tried to smile. "Eulalia Culpepper certainly seems to think so."

To her surprise, he captured her elbows in his hands. "Not talkin' about her but about us. We get on

100

well."

"So we do."

"And I wouldn't want you to think I'm—well, beyond a husband's duties. I'm not." To her increasing astonishment, he drew her forward into his arms. She saw his moustache coming closer, closer to her face, before he very gently laid his lips on hers.

A kiss. A genuine one.

Matthew had kissed her, to be sure. That had been nothing like this. Aggressive and, frankly, full of slobber, it had bordered on the unpleasant.

This—this!

It was warm and titillating. It thrilled her all the way to her toes. And, well, goodness, but Earl tasted good. Who would have thought?

When the kiss ended, he pulled her farther into his arms, right up against him, and whispered in her ear, "What I'm trying to tell you, Miss Vicky, is you make me feel like a young man."

Oh. Oh, goodness. Maybe—maybe she should say yes.

She sincerely believed she could develop feelings for Earl Hanson. Knowing he'd offered for her mostly out of pity just took the shine off it.

She stepped away from him. He let her go immediately. "May I have time, Earl, to consider your offer?"

"Take as much time as you'd like. The offer stands."

"Thank you."

He nodded and fitted his hat on his head. "Just send me a message at the livery."

"Will you be in town for a while?"

"Yes, ma'am." He turned to go, and paused. "If you need anything at all—"

Like your heart? Victoria wondered while he stepped out. What if she wanted his heart?

****

"Take his offer," Tom Morgan said harshly, once he heard about Earl's visit. Victoria had confided in Hattie as soon as Earl left, and when Tom got home from work, Hattie shared the news. "You sure as shootin' won't get another one." Tom raked her up and down. "Not at your age."

"Tom Morgan!" Hattie scolded. "How can you be so rude?"

"No offense," Tom told Victoria, very offensively indeed. "But I've had enough of it. I never wanted her here in the first place."

Victoria, her cheeks burning, said, "I'll pack my things at once, and go."

"Where?" Hattie asked.

Good question. Earl's cabin came to mind—a refuge, and no mistake. But the man came with the dwelling.

You make me feel like a young man. Oh, Lordy. She couldn't…

"Marry the sheriff," Tom urged, seemingly completing Victoria's thought. "It's your best bet."

"Tom," Hattie protested again. "She's paying us rent."

"Haven't seen any of it yet."

"I should get paid tonight. I'll give you my board tomorrow."

"All right, then you can stay here, but just till you decide to take Earl up on his offer, hear?"

What a terrible thing, Victoria grieved as she went up to her room to get ready for the saloon. What a terrible thing to be a woman alone in the world. She shed a tear or two over it while she pinned up her hair. No secure place to lay her head.

And now she had a whole evening to look forward to, alone amid the perils of the Trail's End saloon.

****

"Earl? What are you doing out here in the cold?"

Earl spun on his heel when he heard the question posed behind him. It was a bit nippy out here on the sidewalk in front of the Trail's End saloon, now that he came to think on it. He'd been so focused on listening to what went on inside, he'd barely noticed.

Coyote Sullivan regarded him with a level gaze, his hat pulled down, his collar turned up, and his doctor's bag in his hand.

"Hello, Doc. You going or coming?"

"On my way home. The Taylors' youngest had a fever. It's broken now."

"That's real good."

"But what are you doing out here?" Coyote eyed Earl up and down. "Not exactly good for your knees, is it?"

"Hang my knees. They're fine."

Coyote shifted his weight. "Ya know, I've been hearing a lot about you, around town."

Earl growled. "Like what?"

"Like, you've been having your way with the lady piano player in there." He jerked his thumb at the saloon.

"I have not."

"No? Shame."

Earl growled, more loudly, "It funny to you, Coyote, the prospect of ruinin' a good woman's reputation?"

"Not at all. But she's probably better company than a dog."

"What's that supposed to mean?"

"You said you were lonely. Said you meant to pick up a stray dog."

"I said no such thing."

Coyote grinned. "Question is, why are you out here if she's in there?"

"It's all a misunderstanding."

"So you didn't spend the night with her up at your cabin?"

Earl scowled. "Not the way you're implying."

"I'm implying nothing. You aren't courting her, then?"

"Well, sort of. That was a scheme to get Eulalia Culpepper off my back."

"Yeah? How's it working?"

Earl fought down an impulse to wipe the smirk off Coyote's face. "Go home to your wife," he suggested. "I'll just wait here—"

He broke off as a crash and a tremulous cry sounded from within, cutting through the other racket inside the saloon.

"Hellfire!" Earl shouted, and busted in through the wing doors.

There, chaos reigned. Well, chaos usually did reign inside the Trail's End, but this looked worse than usual. A table had been turned over, cards flung everywhere, and Cory had the shotgun out from behind the bar, balanced in his hands.

Earl turned his gaze to Victoria, who sat cringing behind the piano. Just behind her on the wall, he saw a splashed pattern of whiskey. He knew what that meant—somebody had thrown a bottle, which had shattered.

Just missing her—or so he hoped.

"What's goin' on here?" he roared.

Heads spun toward him, but nobody answered. Didn't have to. He'd broken up enough fights over the years to read this scene accurately. Besides, one man lay sprawled on his back atop the collapsed table and another stood with balled fists and blood running down his chin.

Earl went wading in, and laid what he liked to call the hand of the law on the standing fellow's shoulder, while eyeing the other for signs of serious damage. The sprawled fellow still looked angry, and that meant he was alive.

"What in damnation!" Earl hollered. "Cory?"

"Argument over a card game, Sheriff. Nobody drew a gun 'cept me."

Earl didn't realize Coyote had followed him in till he turned to Victoria and saw the doc there already at her side. When Earl stomped over to the piano, she looked up at him.

"Miss Vicky, you all right?"

She didn't answer. She had her hands clasped together above the keyboard and looked pale as milk.

"Just shaken, I think," Coyote said. "I'll check out that other fellow for injuries." He stepped away, effectively leaving the two of them alone.

Earl fought down his emotions. Behind the chair where Victoria sat, shattered glass covered the floor. He wanted to take her in his arms and comfort her, he did—right there in front of everyone. He longed to touch her, so much it hurt. And in his chest, his heart pounded like the hooves of a wild stallion.

"I'm all right," she croaked, and he didn't believe her. "But that struck so close—"

"It didn't hit you? No cuts?"

"I don't know. There might be some glass in my hair."

A glance told Earl the occupants of the saloon were watching. He didn't care. Stepping close, he saw that the back of Victoria's head glittered.

"Yup. Covered with it. Here, stand up." Very gently, he took her hand. And then, as he'd desired to do since first he saw her, he touched her hair, brushing the glass away as carefully as he could.

She stood quietly beneath his fingers, turned away from the room and half concealed by the high back of the piano. It didn't help. Earl felt riled. Riled in more ways than one. He wanted to protect her. He wanted to rip the heads off those two cowboys for risking her safety.

Instead, he tended her as he would a child and swept up the glass with his own hands. Then he told her to sit back down and called for a whiskey.

"A beer, you mean," Victoria objected.

"You need something stronger than that." He needed one too, but wouldn't say so. He handed her the glass Cory brought over. "Here—sip that."

She sat. She sipped. He had no reason to believe she'd remain so amiable for long.

Sure enough, when he leaned over her and said, "You know, Miss Vicky, this is no fit place for you," her gaze flew to his, and she bristled.

"I have no choice. What else am I supposed to do?"

He looked her in the eye. "Well, I've already made one suggestion."

Her cheeks flushed with heat, not from the whiskey. "Marry you, you mean," she whispered.

"Could be worse." Maybe he was wrong. He made no great prize, despite Eulalia Culpepper's apparent opinion to the contrary. "Almost was."

With considerable dignity, Victoria said, "I am still considering your offer."

"Ah. Well. Good." That meant she hadn't refused him outright. "While you're busy considering, let me see you home."

"Nonsense. I haven't finished my shift."

Stubborn woman.

"Besides, tongues will wag."

"I don't give a buffalo's backside what folks say."

"No?"

"No, ma'am. In fact, if you insist on stayin' here, I'll stay with you."

Before she could protest, he carried over a chair and plunked it down in his old place, beside hers. Settling there, he crossed his arms and planted his feet.

A few catcalls came from the occupants of the saloon. At least Coyote had gone home to that pretty little wife of his.

Earl glared fiercely into the room, silencing the wiseacres. Victoria was here, and here he meant to stay.

Chapter Seventeen

The last thing Victoria wanted, after her shattering day and even more shattering evening, was a lecture. But that's just what Earl offered her while he walked her home, after the saloon closed.

The night was quiet, or as quiet as it ever got in Wylder. Voices and snatches of song echoed along the street—the last tune she'd played—but the wind was quiet, and no snow or sleet beat at her head.

She listened patiently to Earl, right up until the moment he declared, "That there saloon is no proper place for a lady like you, Miss Victoria."

She turned on him. "And who are you, Earl Hanson, to tell me my place?"

He blinked at her, looking like a man who'd just been attacked by a fluffy kitten.

"I'm not—"

"You most certainly are. Tell me, is that what marriage means to you? That you can start making decisions as to what your woman does and thinks?"

"Well, now." He backed off a careful step. "It's a long time since I been married."

"If that's what's in your head, you can just forget it. I'm an independent woman, and I need to make a living."

He smiled, actually smiled. That moustache of his twitched, and even in the dark street, she saw his eyes light.

"Earl Hanson, are you laughing at me?"

"No, ma'am."

"Then what's that grin about?"

"Just thinking there ain't nothing like a redheaded woman."

"Then you'd better go court Mrs. Culpepper." Victoria started walking again.

"Now, Victoria. Here, stop." He caught her shoulders. He did it gently, but it halted her in her tracks.

"Victoria," he said softly, "sure, you know I'm just worried about you. If that bottle had hit you instead of the wall, back there tonight—"

Victoria melted. It might be his tone of voice or the way he was looking at her, but all her anger magically evaporated.

"I know. And it's good of you to be concerned. But if marriage means losing my say—"

"It doesn't. especially not at our stage of life. Not sure I'd want a wife who was all obedient." He began lacing his fingers through her hair.

"Earl? What are you doing?"

"Just checking for more pieces of glass."

Yet his fingers dug deep and, oh, it was a marvelous sensation, one that caused her to step closer and lift her face to his.

He mused, "Not sure I like obedience. I want a little bit o' fire."

With that, he kissed her. Again. Right there in the street, he did.

Victoria's mind shattered. This wasn't like the other kiss, which had been careful, even respectful.

This one captured her and drew her in. It—well, it contained fire, just as he'd said.

Victoria flailed wildly between the need to step away and the desire to do anything but. She hadn't expected such desire.

Not, as he said, at her stage of life.

His moustache felt soft, and it tickled. His lips, though, conveyed a powerful amount of emotion. And when the kiss ended, she collapsed in his arms.

"Marry me, Vicky," he whispered in her ear. "Marry me, and I'll let you do whatever you want."

Well, that certainly left things wide open. What she wanted right now was to kiss him again. But even if she was inexperienced at playing this game, she knew a woman didn't tip her hand.

"I told you, Earl, I'm considering."

"Consider a bit faster." He nuzzled her cheek, and she turned her face so her lips brushed his. She said, "This is highly improper. We can't stand here in the street like this. If Tom finds out—"

"Right, you're right. But promise me you'll consider with some speed."

Victoria giggled, she actually did, a remarkable thing after the terrible night she'd had. Standing here in the cold with Earl made her feel—well, not terrible at all. Alive, and as if she mattered.

The shocking thought occurred to her: *Maybe she should marry him.*

Instead, she asked with surprising coyness, "Will you be at the Trail's End tomorrow night?"

"If you want me there."

"Sitting beside me, like a guard?"

"If it wouldn't trample too hard on your

independence."

"Maybe if we play a few songs together, folks will think you're just there for the entertainment."

"I'll be there, then. And Victoria?"

"Yes?"

He kissed her once more, this one soft and yet potent enough to set her legs to trembling. "Something to help you think."

****

Earl woke in Ulysses' stall with his knees aching to beat the band and Victoria on his mind.

It seemed, in fact, as if she'd been with him all through his slumber, so she was already there when he opened his eyes. The way she looked at him with that luminous gaze. The way she tasted on his tongue. The feel of her between his hands…

He rose with a groan and a hand to his back. These nights spent in the straw would likely kill him. He needed his own bed. *He needed Victoria in his bed.*

That thought startled him so much, he swore under his breath. What in holy hell had got into him?

It had been a long time, he thought as he stumbled outside, since he'd been married. And Little Bird had been a completely different proposition from Victoria Major.

He'd met her father, an Oglala Sioux, while trapping. When White Eagle took him home, Little Bird had flirted with him, giggled, and made eyes. She was scarcely more than a girl then, innocent and used to following her father's will.

Though her decision to come away with Earl had been her own.

She'd never bucked his decisions, even though

they weren't what you'd call officially married. He'd called her wife, and she'd called him husband. Young and strong as he was back in those days, it hadn't taken him long to get his babe inside her.

She'd lost the first child, which should have warned him. And the second. After some seven years together, the third had come to term, only to die in a welter of blood along with Little Bird.

A son. Another Hanson, one who would never see the world.

Damn it all, he thought as he stumbled outside. Why would he think of that now? He hadn't thumbed over that sorrow for some time, had tucked it away and damn near forgotten it.

Only he hadn't forgotten. A man could never forget such a thing—burying the woman and child he loved—unless he was made of stone.

Had he loved Little Bird? Well, sure. He'd loved her giggle, her sweet nature, and her lovely, dark eyes. Losing her had stung him so he'd never loved again.

Until now?

Standing at the split rail fence outside the livery, he stared at nothing while he considered that question as honestly as he could. Because a man needed to be honest about matters of the heart.

Even if that required a certain amount of courage.

Did he have that kind of courage? He would have said so. But now the thought of Victoria Major scared him. It scared him more than the prospect of a wounded grizzly bear.

Chapter Eighteen

Victoria's step faltered when she entered the mercantile and saw Eulalia Culpepper there ahead of her. In fact, she heard the woman's voice even before she caught sight of her. Eulalia stood across the counter from Finn Wylder, holding forth in a manner that had caught the attention of most everyone there.

"—shocking, I call it!" she declared as Victoria went in. "For a man of his reputation to step so far outside the bounds of common decency. Like a—a common lowlife."

A few of her listeners nodded. Finn Wylder, whom Victoria considered a fair man, held up a hand. "Now, Eulalia—Earl Hanson's a good fellow."

All the breath rushed from Victoria's lungs, just as if she'd been struck in the gut. Oh, no. Oh—

Eulalia rounded on the shopkeeper. "He used to be. I'll give you that, Finn Wylder. He used to be an honorable man, the kind with whom a lady would be proud to associate. Now he spends every night in the lowest saloon in Wylder, with that woman. That—that—"

Heads were turning in Victoria's direction. A murmur started up, somebody telling Eulalia Culpepper that the object of her disgust—one object of it, at least—was here. Victoria wanted to fall through the plank floor. She wanted to turn and run away, but she seemed frozen by her dismay.

Besides, would she allow herself to be chased away by the likes of Eulalia Culpepper? Meeting the woman's eyes, like two hard marbles, her heart quailed within her. *Yes.*

"A decent woman," Eulalia declared still more loudly, "wouldn't take a job in a saloon. She wouldn't swig beer all night like a sailor. And she certainly wouldn't lead a good man astray."

Her listeners there in the mercantile drew a collective breath. Then, somewhat in the manner of the Red Sea, they parted, leaving a clear path between Eulalia and Victoria, for Eulalia's ire to travel. And, ire it was. Victoria felt it strike her in the face, an attack on her defenses.

Frail as they were.

"You should be ashamed," Eulalia told Victoria. "Given what you've done."

"What I've done?" Victoria repeated uncertainly.

"Seducing a good man, as I say. Spending the night alone with him, at his cabin. Yes, everybody in town knows. You're a trollop, that's what. A trollop and a hussy."

Victoria wanted to deny it. As she stood there in her high-necked, dark blue gown, she wondered how she could look less like a hussy. Yet—well, it sounded so bad, the way Eulalia put it. And scandal did seem to follow her, mad as that idea might be.

She lifted her chin a notch and said, "You tell me what's worse, a hussy or a sour-tongued old prune who goes around spreading false rumors."

"Prune?" Eulalia clearly enjoyed tossing mud, but not being on the receiving end of a toss. She glanced around at the townsfolk, who still listened avidly. "I should think the answer to that is plain. I'm a respectable widow. And you—well, there's only one way you could attract a man like Earl Hanson."

Those words struck Victoria even more forcefully than the pious ones that had preceded them. Maybe because she believed they were true. Well past her bloom and plain as molasses. Had she ever imagined anything different?

"Excuse me," she murmured before turning around abruptly. Back down the steps of the mercantile she went, stumbling out into the street, where the air seemed to dance around her. It took her several minutes to realize it was snowing.

She needed to go home. Only she didn't have a home, not really. She could no longer remember why she'd entered the mercantile, and anyway, she needed to pack.

She needed to pack so she could be on the very next conveyance out of Wylder.

****

"Victoria? Victoria, please open the door." Hattie had knocked softly at first. Now her inquiries turned urgent. "What's happened? What's wrong? Victoria, I can hear you crying."

Victoria got up from the bed, clutching a handkerchief that had soaked through, and unlocked the door. Hattie eyed her from a face full of concern. "What is it? Are you ill?"

"No. I'm leaving." Victoria waved at her satchel, which sat on the foot of the bed. Hard to believe everything she owned fit in that small bag.

"Leaving?" Hattie repeated. "If you're worried

about Tom, he'll come round."

"It's not that. Oh, I have your board money." Victoria dug in her change purse. "I did get paid last night. Give this to Tom, please, and tell him I won't trouble him any longer."

"But, Victoria, where will you go?"

"I haven't decided yet." The tears in Victoria's eyes spilled over yet again. "Back east. I don't belong out here."

"You sure about that? What about Earl?"

Pain pierced Victoria's heart. "What about him?"

"I'm pretty sure you have feelings for him, and he for you."

"I'm certain all he feels for me is pity. And a woman doesn't want pity from the man she...admires. Hattie, the people here in Wylder despise me. I can't do that to him."

"Earl Hanson's a strong sort of man. I suspect he can stick up for himself."

Victoria ignored that. "The train stops here in Wylder tomorrow. I'm planning to be on it. I'll tell Mr. Callahan tonight."

"And Earl? You going to tell him also?"

Victoria thought about it and shook her head. "Better not. He'll—he'll forget all about me once I'm gone."

"You're sure about that, too?"

Victoria nodded. She didn't dare face Earl again. And it was best to leave now while she still owned a few scraps of her heart.

****

She arrived at the Trail's End early, so she could talk to Mr. Callahan. He stood behind the bar, and she asked for a minute of his time. They stepped away to the piano.

"Mr. Callahan, I'm handing in my notice as of tonight."

"What?"

"Quitting. I'm quitting."

"Well, Miss Major, I'm sorry to hear that. From what Cory says, you were settling in well. And the customers have nearly stopped complaining."

There was a recommendation!

"Did you find another job?"

"No, sir. I've decided to leave Wylder."

"Really?" His eyebrows twitched. "You tell Earl that?"

"It has nothing to do with Mr. Hanson. And I'd really rather not involve him in my business."

Mr. Callahan looked unhappy. "I don't like the idea of lyin' to Earl."

"I'm not asking you to lie to him. If you see him, just don't mention a small detail."

"Small," Callahan grumped.

"Mr. Callahan, this isn't your problem." Victoria tipped up her chin. "Or your business."

He nodded miserably. "Well, then, I'll just clear out of here, so my tongue won't run away with me."

"And I'll go play some popular tunes."

The saloon had filled up by the time Earl rolled in carrying the old six-string guitar. He grinned at Victoria, the luxurious moustache twitching and, damn it all, as easy as that, her heart fluttered.

"Evening, Miss Vicky."

Miss Vicky. Would she ever be able to hear her name again without remembering the way he said it?

117

Oh, heavens, she was going to lose her composure right here, in front of him.

Somehow, she managed to smile. "Evening."

"Hope you don't mind I brought Louise. Thought we might play a few songs together."

"I'd like that." Even if it was for the last time.

He eased into his chair beside hers, which nobody had bothered to move, and gave her one of those bright blue stares. "Everything all right?"

No. Most definitely not.

"I guess I'm just a little nervous. It's busy in here tonight."

"Don't worry." He laid his hand on her knee and squeezed gently. "I got your back."

And, quite possibly, her heart.

"You playing tonight, Sheriff?" a passerby asked.

"He ain't the sheriff," Victoria answered, and they both laughed.

****

The night wound down slowly as the drunks and other regulars went home. A good night, and no mistake. Songs, warmth, laughter.

And Earl was pretty sure he'd made progress talking Miss Vicky round.

Something seemed different, that was for certain. She kept giving him soft glances—wistful ones—and when a woman took to looking at a man that way, Earl figured it meant she welcomed his presence in her life.

Yeah, for sure he was wearing her down.

He couldn't wait to walk her home and maybe snatch another of those sweet kisses, the ones that kept him warm all night. Maybe he could just persuade an answer out of her—a *yes*.

They walked slowly through a night clear and cold. Earl found himself thinking about the cabin, how different it would feel with Miss Vicky installed there, making the place complete. Making it a home.

Yep, sure enough, she was all he needed.

"Miss Vicky—" At the Morgans' door, they turned to face one another. "I sure did enjoy this evening."

"I did too, Earl. Very much." She laid her hand on his arm, as if she claimed him. Just like he belonged to her.

He did, he did.

"Funny, Miss Vicky, when I'm with you—well, I don't feel like a retired sheriff. I feel like the young buck I used to be. The one with the wild heart. I guess he's still here, inside o' me. And you—you bring him out."

Quite a speech for him, who didn't use a lot of words. He hoped she understood what he meant.

Maybe so, because she kind of leaned in to him, all trusting.

He kissed her gently, thoroughly, feeling the staggering rightness of it. His heart—quiet for so long in its prison—beat against his ribs like, well, just like a wild thing.

"Miss Vicky," he whispered then, "you have an answer for me yet?"

"Oh, Earl." Was she crying? She trapped his face between her hands and kissed him again, a kiss that surely tasted of devotion. But she said, "Not yet. Not yet."

"All right." He fought down his disappointment. He wanted her in his life, wanted to hold her in his arms all night, and he wanted to make love to her, damn it.

"I—I'd better go in." Yet she hung onto him.

"One more kiss?"

She gave it readily, but when she moved out of his arms and went inside, he felt sure she was crying.

Almost, almost he rapped on the door behind her. But he didn't want to rouse the house so late.

Something was wrong. Suddenly he believed that all the way down to his toes. He just didn't know what.

Chapter Nineteen

Earl heard the whistle from the train the next morning, when he staggered out late. Must be leaving the station, he thought with the former-sheriff portion of his mind that still insisted on keeping track of such things.

It had started snowing, tiny flakes that swirled down from a dead-white sky, promising more. His knees complained, and his very bones ached as he stumped up to the split rail fence outside the livery. Ulysses was already in the paddock and came over to visit with him.

"Hello, old man." Earl caressed the big horse's nose. "You lookin' for some exercise? Maybe later, once I get this old body o' mine movin' properly."

Buck Standish came by, his black head bare and collecting snowflakes. Buck used to help in the livery, before he quit to work full-time at his wife's business, the Wylder Side Bakery.

He nodded at Earl. "Sheriff."

"Haven't you been told? I ain't the sheriff no more."

Buck strolled up, looking curious. "Seems like you're making offers of marriage instead."

"What?" Earl stared at him. "Where'd you hear that?"

"It's all over town. Way I heard it, Tom Morgan

said his boarder would be moving out of his place soon as she marries you—like you asked her."

Earl's heart leaped. Did that mean Victoria had made up her mind? Or was Tom Morgan just blowing smoke?

"Uh—I asked her, sure. She hasn't given me her answer yet."

Buck's dark eyes went serious. "I'm happy for you, Sher—Earl. But I think you might want to know, I just saw your lady friend—Miss Major, isn't it?—getting on the train."

Earl stared at Standish. "You must be mistaken."

"Tall lady, kinda slender, red hair—the one who plays piano in the saloon?"

"Yep."

"You might want to get moving, then, Earl, and try to stop her. 'Cause I did see her boarding, and she had a satchel."

"Damnation!" Earl bellowed, and ran.

He ran even though he couldn't remember the last time he'd done so. His fear overcame the protest put up by his knees, and after a minute they gave in, and went along with it. He reached the station just in time to see the train pull away.

Too late. He was too damn late.

Pain erupted in his chest so, for a minute, he thought he was dying. Right here in Wylder, with the snow coming down.

Then he caught sight of the ticket master, turned, and laid hold of him. "Is Miss Major on that train? Middle-aged lady. Red hair."

The man goggled at him. "Yes, I think so. Let go, you're choking me!"

122

Earl let go. Hell, what to do? He could think of only one thing—in fact his whole spirit and a considerable amount of libido urged him to it.

He'd have to give Ulysses the exercise the old horse craved.

****

There weren't a lot of passengers on the train. Victoria had a seat all to herself, which suited her just fine. She didn't want to garner any attention when the tears came, and she knew they would. Already she fought them. As the train pulled away from Wylder, it felt as if she'd left a part of her behind.

That was because she'd left her heart there, in Wylder. She tried to determine when it had passed into Earl Hanson's keeping. Had it been the first time he came to her rescue? The first time she'd been on the receiving end of his smile? The first time he kissed her?

No—no, it had been the music that drew her to him, the hours spent playing together with easy abandon, that turned what should have been a purgatory in the Trail's End Saloon to blissful harmony.

Never before had she been in love. She had only a vague notion what it meant. But snaring the object of her affection out of sheer obligation didn't fit with any of her notions. And Earl had only proposed to her out of a sense of duty—nothing more.

If she thought there was something more, if she believed he cared for her one jot as much as she cared for him...why, she'd haul this train to a screeching halt and run back, run straight into his arms.

But the train had now reached full speed and steamed eastward. Outside Victoria's window, the snow fell faster, making a lacy white curtain on the glass.

One through which she could see ranches and farmsteads passing by, countryside patched in green and white, places where folks who cared for one another lived out their lives.

And a man on a large brown horse.

Victoria blinked and leaned toward the window, straining for a better look. The horse and rider traveled in the same direction as the train, and the horse ran flat out, making the most of its long stride. The man on its back must be an expert rider, for he lay along the neck of his mount, his very posture urging the animal on.

Victoria caught her breath in wonder and admiration, for she saw something marvelous in the pair, a wildness that could never be tamed. She also saw a certain familiarity…

Who was he? Surely she knew that horse, so big, brown, and rawboned.

Other passengers on her side of the train had now caught sight of the pair, and began to exclaim. Folks from the other side of the aisle stood up and peered out, one gentleman who smelled strongly of bay rum using Victoria's window.

"What's happening?" she asked him.

"I do believe that fellow's trying to catch the train."

"Why?"

Before the man could answer, the brown horse gained ground. It looked like the rider meant to pass the steaming engine. A mad thing to do, entirely!

Cursing the snowflakes now, and brushing ineffectually at the glass, Victoria heard someone behind her cry, "Train robbery! That fella's gonna hold up the train!"

Folks all over the passenger car exclaimed. Gentlemen drew their firearms. Women shrieked. People leaped up from their seats.

The conductor appeared from forward.

"What's happenin', Jim?" someone called.

"Everybody keep calm. Engineer will outrun that robber. If—"

He got no farther before a shot rang out. Even damped by the sound of the engine, there could be no mistaking it.

The train immediately slowed. Victoria pressed her face against the chilly glass, but she could no longer see the brown horse.

Brown horse. Tall and rawboned.

By God, that was Ulysses! And that meant the rider must be—

She stumbled to her feet even as the train, puffing madly, ground to a halt there on the tracks. Snow fell thickly now outside the windows, and Victoria discovered she still possessed her heart after all. It pounded wildly in her chest.

Shouts came from forward. The train shuddered a bit, and the conductor hollered at Victoria. "Ma'am, you better sit down."

"But—" The word trembled on her lips.

"We bein' robbed?" a man asked again.

A commotion came from the front of the car where somebody—the rider?—argued with the engineer. A man appeared in the doorway, looking oversized.

The shoulders of his coat were white with snow, as was his hat. Victoria knew that hat. Just as she knew the silver moustache and those impossibly blue eyes.

He'd drawn his gun and held it in his right hand.

People exclaimed as he came striding down the aisle of the passenger car.

"Sheriff Hanson?" the conductor cried in amazement.

"I ain't the sheriff no more!" Earl bellowed. He didn't so much as glance at the man or at anyone else in the car. Except Victoria. His gaze fixed upon her, and she went hot and cold by turns.

Oh. Oh!

"Miss Vicky." He shoved his pistol back in the holster with practiced ease.

The engineer appeared behind him. "Mister, if this ain't a train robbery, I—"

"It ain't a train robbery," Earl answered.

"Then what in tarnation you doin' holding up my train? I have a schedule to keep."

"And I got something to take care of. Won't take but a minute."

Earl had reached Victoria's seat now. His gaze still held her captive where she stood trembling. This couldn't, *couldn't* be what it seemed. Earl Hanson hadn't possibly ridden down the train and held it up solely so he could see her. And keep her from leaving...

He swept the hat from his head, and his silvery hair fell over his brow. He looked impossibly large there in the narrow aisle, and overwhelmingly vital.

"Miss Vicky," he said, and his gaze spoke to her even more eloquently than his words. "Why didn't you tell me last night you meant to leave?"

Victoria shook her head, not sure she still possessed a voice.

"Don't matter," Earl decided. "I came to tell you—

126

Don't go. I came to ask you—"

He reached out and took her hand. As he did, he shifted his weight and, right there in the narrow aisle, went down on one knee.

Victoria gasped.

"Miss Vicky, you make me feel—but I'm not sure there are words. You make me feel like a young man again. But not stupid, like I was when I was young and dumb. Oh hell, I'm messing this up."

"You're not." Victoria's eyes flooded with tears.

"What I'm tryin' to say is, you've showed me my heart is still a young man's heart, same as it was."

"Young and wild," Victoria said.

"Wild," he agreed, and the spark of a smile came into his eyes. "Only I reckon it belongs to you now. If you'll accept it."

"Oh, Earl!"

"I love you, Victoria Major. Stay. Stay and marry me."

"Oh, Earl!" she cried again, and launched herself forward into his arms. Did he rise from the floor of the train, or did she pull him up? It didn't matter, once his arms closed around her. He smelled of the cold and of horse, and of—of belonging. The place she wanted to be.

"Yes?" he asked. "Do you say yes?"

"Yes!"

All around them, the other passengers cheered. And right in front of them, Earl kissed her. The kind of kiss that told her what was in his heart.

"I love you, Victoria," he whispered it this time, into her ear.

"I love you." Words she'd never said before.

"This is all very pretty," the engineer butted in.

"And romantic," said a female passenger, her hands clasped to her chest.

"And romantic," the engineer allowed. "But I still have a schedule to keep."

"Sorry about that." Earl clasped his hat back on his head amid a little shower of snowflakes. "We're gettin' off here. Got a wedding to plan, back in Wylder."

The conductor slapped him on the back. Earl snatched up Victoria's satchel and escorted her back up the aisle and out into a world of white.

Ulysses stood there, though Victoria could barely see him through the whirling snowflakes. Earl jumped down from the train and Victoria leaped into his arms.

Symbolic, that, since she leaped clear into a new life. One of long days full of shared music and laughter. Even longer nights, sharing warmth and love.

The engine fired up, and Earl led her away from the train. As it began to chug away, slow at first and then faster and faster, he kissed her again, with the snowflakes pattering against her cheek.

"We'll have to take it slow," he said when the kiss ended.

"I think we'd better," she breathed.

He laughed unsteadily. "I meant, the trip back to Wylder. Ulysses is about winded. And I ain't as young as I used to be. You sure you want an old, used-up ex-sheriff?"

"I want you, Earl. And you were magnificent."

"Magnificent, eh?" He quirked a brow. "Little lady, you ain't seen nothing yet."

Epilog

Victoria rose with the dawn and left the warmth of the bed to tiptoe across the chilly, wide-plank floor. Outside the cabin, snow tumbled down and a deer grazed, pawing the white ground with a delicate hoof. No—that was an elk. Earl had taught her how to tell the difference.

He'd already taught her so many things— especially on their wedding night, last night.

She turned her head to look at him where he lay, still asleep in the big brass bed. Earl's bed no longer. Now it had become *their* bed, where they shared so much loving and the kind of deep connection she'd never even hoped to experience.

She was a woman after all. Maybe even a wild woman.

Oh, what had she done to deserve such a man? Strong. Gentle. And so romantic.

Just remembering how romantic had her tingling from head to toe. Or maybe that was the cold. She'd better hop on back into bed.

Oh, yes, she'd better.

On a rising surge of joy, she sprinted back to the bed and dove beneath the eiderdown. Earl's arms came out and welcomed her.

He murmured, "There's my girl."

"Girl?" She giggled. Not hardly, but he did make

her feel like one, new, and oh, so beautiful.

Maybe here, in their private kingdom, they would become what they'd always been meant to be. Her—not a spectator but a woman living her life by choice, the choice of love. Him, not an ex-sheriff but a man who pledged himself to that woman with all his being.

Earl ran his fingers through her hair and nuzzled her neck.

"My wife."

"Yes."

Here, alone together, they were just Victoria and Earl, ageless in their love, and forever wild.

A word about the author...

Multi-award-winning author Laura Strickland delights in time traveling to the past and searching out settings for her books, be they Historical Romance, Steampunk, or something in between. Her first Scottish Historical hero, Devil Black, battled his way onto the publishing scene in 2013, and the author never looked back.

Nor has she tapped the limits of her imagination. Venturing beyond Historical and Contemporary Romance, she created a new world with her ground-breaking Buffalo Steampunk Adventure series set in her native city in Western New York.

Married and the parent of one grown daughter, Laura has also been privileged to mother a number of very special rescue dogs, and is intensely interested in animal welfare. Her love of dogs, and her lifelong interest in Celtic history, magic and music, are all reflected in her writing. Laura's mantra is Lore, Legend, Love, and she wouldn't have it any other way.

Thank you for purchasing
this publication of The Wild Rose Press, Inc.

For questions or more information
contact us at
info@thewildrosepress.com.

The Wild Rose Press, Inc.
www.thewildrosepress.com

www.ingramcontent.com/pod-product-compliance
Lightning Source LLC
Chambersburg PA
CBHW072001170626
46813CB00005B/1957